I0600548

Bradford Kuhn

# THE GATEKEEPER

STORMSHIELD
PUBLISHING

This book is a work of fiction. Any references to historical events, real people, or real places are used fictitiously. Other names, characters, places, and events are products of the author's imagination, and any resemblance to actual events or places or persons, living or dead, is entirely coincidental.

Copyright 2025 by Bradford Kuhn. All rights reserved, including the right to reproduce this book or portions thereof in any form whatsoever.

Published by Stormshield Publishing.

Interior design by Inksnatcher.

Cover illustration by Mandy O'Brien of https://www.larkandwren.com/

Printed in the United States of America.

Library of Congress Cataloging-in-Publication Data

Names: Kuhn, Bradford, author

Title: The Gatekeeper/Bradford Kuhn

Subjects: | BISAC: FICTION/Fantasy/Action & Adventure. FICTION/Fantasy/Epic. FICTION/Fantasy/Paranormal.

Description: First e-book edition. | Stormshield Publishing, 2025. | Summary: "When a wounded stranger collapses on his doorstep, solitary John is thrust into a perilous world of magic, deception, and destiny as the reluctant guardian of a powerful gem." — Provided by publisher.

Identifiers: LCCN 2025907894 | ISBN 979-8-9929956-0-2 (paperback) | ISBN 979-8-9929956-2-6 (e-book)

LC record available at https://lccn.loc.gov/

For information about special discounts for bulk purchases, or if you'd like the author to speak at your event, please contact the author via bradford.renwick.kuhn@gmail.com.

*To my mom, who was there encouraging me throughout the whole writing process.*

# 1

Horses' footfalls echoed down the valley, and John's knife paused midair, a flake of wood from his whittling drifting to the ground. He glanced up the gray stone pathway, barely wide enough for a wagon. Hooves clattered rhythmically, coming ever closer to his log cabin, tucked at the foot of a cliff.

John slid his knife into the sheath he kept on his waist. Horses meant money, and money meant trouble. He grabbed his bow from its spot against the wall and slung it over his head. Reaching over to his quiver, he grabbed a fully whittled arrow, hesitated, then tied the quiver onto his belt. He hastily attempted to smooth down his hair into something resembling order, then patted his well-trimmed beard.

He saw the rider first, then the horse's head, as the figure crested the hill. A woman! Dressed in white with vines of green dancing across her clothes, a hood covering her head, she was slumped over the horse's neck, as if exhausted. John relaxed, watching the white horse trot forward.

"Ma'am," John said, with a small nod. With every step the horse took, the woman seemed to slouch farther.

"Ma'am?" John walked toward her.

She fell to the ground with a soft thump. He broke into a run.

The horse tossed its head and whinnied as John skidded to a stop beside it. At that point, John saw the blood.

He sprinted into his cabin, ripped open a dresser drawer, and grabbed a clean shirt—the nice one that Anderson insisted he buy but he never wore. Dashing back outside, he pressed the garment into the rider's stomach wound with both hands and watched as the shirt turned red. John clenched his jaw and kept the pressure on the wound as blood pooled on the stone beneath her. What started as a stream quickly turned into a trickle, and finally the flow of blood stopped. With one hand on the wound, John secured the makeshift bandage with his belt and lifted the woman into his arms.

John maneuvered the bloody package through the doorway, careful not to bump her head, and made his way to his bed, which was little more than an elevated slab with a sack of feathers on it. Laying her down gently, he stood with a sigh to take his first good look at her. Her skin was darker than his, a creamy brown. An obsidian-black ponytail reached to her waist. She resembled a statue one might find at a rich merchant's house—hosting an aura of age but without the wrinkles, unlike John's sun-browned face with its premature crinkles around the eyes.

"Well, shit," he said to himself, gazing at the woman. She was still breathing but maybe not for long. His eyes locked onto the crest on her chest—a top view of a red rose. Beneath the crest was writing in an unfamiliar language. He stroked the cloth on her sleeve between his fingers, feeling the fine weave. A faint perfume aroma almost masked the scent of blood.

"I don't suppose you are just a rich merchant, huh?" John asked the unconscious woman. "Of course not," he added.

With another heavy sigh, he stepped out of the cabin. The sun was now past its zenith. "Hey, horse," John said, in what he hoped was a reassuring tone. The animal nibbled the grass sprouting between the stones in front of the house. "Hey, uh, horse," John spoke again, taking a cautious step forward. The horse raised its head to stare.

"Hey. Uh, Anderson is in town. But it's a bit of a walk to get there," John said, taking another careful step. "And, well …" John added. Another step. The horse went back to eating. "See, I could walk, but it would take a while for me to get to Anderson. He's a doctor, you see. From the city and everything. Smart guy. Takes care of everyone around here."

John crept to within an arm's reach of the horse. As the horse took another big bite of grass, chewing it nonchalantly, John reached for the saddle.

The horse stopped and snorted at him, stomping one of his large hooves. John hesitated for one more moment, then grabbed a strap. The horse lunged at him, snapping his teeth together a few inches from John's face.

John stumbled backward. "Look, I'm trying to get help for her, okay? Calm down." He reached for the strap again. The horse glared but permitted him to grab it. Nervously, John put his foot in the stirrup and began mounting, before realizing he had put the wrong foot in. "Ah, it's been a while." At last, he mounted as the horse stared over its shoulder at him.

"Where are your reins? Where is your bit?" John asked the horse, who just snorted at him. He settled for grabbing its mane. "Uh. Hyah? Hup?" he said. The horse started at a trot and soon broke into a gallop, John's fingers twisted into the mane so tightly, he feared the circulation might cut off.

~

The horse thundered down the road. The trip to Broken Farm Valley normally took John an hour. Now, John raised his eyebrows in surprise when horse and rider crested the hill in far less time. The cracked fertility pillar, overgrown with vines, came into view. He tried nudging the horse to the other side of the road, eager to give it a wide berth, but to no avail. He settled for leaning away as they rode past. Storm had long since drained from the stone, but it still made John uneasy.

The countryside changed from forest to farm fields, each with its own functional fertility stone—a large obelisk with intricate carvings, humming with Storm. Over the next rise, the village came into view—a cluster of houses dominated by the Storm Church in the center. Its protective wall was simply a ditch with dirt piled behind it. The drawbridge hadn't been raised in years. Horse and rider thundered across it.

John slapped the horse with this hand. "Wait, stop stop stop." As soon as the horse responded to his order, John flung himself out of the saddle, his foot tangling again in the stirrup. "Anderson!" he yelled, hopping on one foot. "Anderson!" Around him, a confused crowd gathered.

"What?" Anderson stepped around the side of the house, white hair shining in the sun, trowel in hand. "I was in the ... That's a warhorse," he finished, pointing at the horse with a dirty trowel.

John finally got his foot free, nearly face-planting into the cobblestones. "Yeah, it belongs to the noble. She's dying in my bed right now. I need help."

"What noble?" Anderson moved toward the door.

"The one in my house," John answered. "Wait, there is one road between here and there, how did you miss her?"

"What's wrong with her?" Anderson yelled from inside.

John leaned in the doorway. "Stomach wound! Lots of blood!"

"Got my kit." Anderson dashed back out, Elizabeth, his wife, at his heels.

"Hold up!" she cried, holding out a hand. "Spectacles." Anderson grabbed them and hung them around his neck.

"Thanks, honey," Anderson said. She kissed his bearded cheek.

John grabbed the doctor's arm and began power walking to the stable. "Take this horse. It's already saddled up."

At this, the horse made a low, dangerous grunt.

"Whoa there," John said, patting it gently. "This is the doc I told you about."

The creature huffed but allowed Anderson to mount.

"Where are the reins?" The old man glanced around.

"Just grab the mane, that's what I did," John said.

"Someone grab me my reins and a bit!" Anderson directed at the crowd that had gathered.

"Horse, just go back to my place." John patted the horse again. It looked straight at him for a second, then took off at a trot. Anderson lurched forward, clutching the mane.

"Out of the way!" John yelled, waving his arms.

The crowd parted as the horse sped to a gallop. "Don't worry, Anderson, the horse knows what he's doing!" John yelled at the rapidly disappearing horse, who quickly outstripped the few figures chasing after it with a bit and reins.

Elizabeth gently poked John in the shoulder. "Do you want to stay the night?"

"Nah, I'll just walk back."

She patted his arm. "Let me get the cart ready, and I'll take you."

John opened his mouth to refuse, then saw the look on her face and closed it. "Yes ma'am," he said with a sigh.

They rode in silence for some time, until Elizabeth decided to update John on the local nobility. As the sun set, John pretended to listen as she finished her story about some child born out of wedlock. They pulled up to his cottage. Outside, the white horse nibbled grass.

John entered, knocking gently on the doorframe. Anderson, slumped in John's chair, roused.

"Hey." Anderson rubbed his eyes with one hand.

"How is she?" John glanced at the swaddled figure on the bed. He noticed a heap of bloody fabric on the table. "You took her clothes off."

"Yeah, I had to treat the wound." Anderson raised an eyebrow. John blushed, scratched his beard, and looked away.

"She's in bad shape," Anderson added.

"Here. Eat." Elizabeth held up a bag.

Anderson took the bag. "She has a fever. She was shivering earlier. It's probably sepsis from the stomach wound."

"What happened?" Elizabeth asked.

"Looks like an animal attack."

"Wolf?" John asked.

Anderson shook his head. "No, that's the strange thing. It looks almost like a bear or a mountain lion with the claw marks. But ..." He paused with a piece of jerky halfway to his mouth. "I've seen animal attacks before. This is ... different."

John broke the silence first. "It was probably a Twisted."

Both Anderson and his wife flinched.

Elizabeth peeked at the woman's face. "She's not local."

"So she's not the count's daughter?" John asked.

"No," Elizabeth said firmly.

"Then who is she?"

While Anderson finished eating, Elizabeth and John examined the woman's belongings on the table: the bloody clothes, a sword, a white cylinder, and a pile of jewelry. One necklace contained a red gem the size of an eyeball. John held up the cylinder. "I think this is a whistle." He blew into one end, and a shrill note sounded.

A shadow appeared in the doorway, snorting at them. The horse eyed them briefly, then returned to his grazing. "Well-trained horse," John muttered. "Why isn't it hurt?"

"Someone or something must have attacked her on foot," Anderson said.

"Do we load her into the cart now?" John asked.

"I want to avoid moving her as much as we can. She's in a bad way." Anderson frowned. "You didn't happen to bring a stretcher?"

"No ..." Elizabeth murmured.

"Don't worry about it; this was all pretty hectic. It will be dark soon, and I don't want to do this at night. Let's go home, get what we need, and return at first light tomorrow. Once we load her up, we can make the trip all the way to the city straight from here."

John stared at the unconscious woman. "What do you need me to do with her?"

"Well, if she wakes up, make sure she doesn't move. Give her water, but no food. Keep her warm, that's important. Try to keep the fire going. That's about it. Do you want Elizabeth to stay?" His wife nodded.

"You're going to need her help to pack," John said.

Anderson sighed. "Are you sure you will be all right alone?"

"Yeah, I'll be fine. Go get ready for tomorrow."

Anderson nodded. "Keep your door closed, just in case."

"Twisted don't come here, you know that. They don't like the rocks around here."

"Yeah, well ..."

"I'll be fine," John said. "I'll keep the fire going."

"All right. I'll see you tomorrow. She ... isn't looking good." Grim faced, Anderson and Elizabeth left.

He couldn't sleep.

Although his bed wasn't all that comfortable, it was slightly better than the floor. Not only was the wounded woman occupying his bed, but all his blankets were also keeping her warm. On top of it, her whimpering—imagined or real—kept him on alert.

He could have imagined it, of course. Maybe he slipped into sleep and his dreams bled into reality. No matter how much he tried to convince himself that it was his imagination, he couldn't. So he sat in his chair and watched her sleep. He had already organized her jewelry and put it all into his lockbox, and gathered firewood for the night. There wasn't much else to do, so he just sat.

A sliver of new moon pierced the night sky. The fire cast a flickering illumination around the small room, barely revealing the woman. Outside, the horse whinnied, scarcely audible over the wind, but something deep inside John took note.

He lit a rushlight, a small, woven wick he'd soaked in fat that gave off a faint glow. He strung his bow and grabbed his quiver before he crept out of his cottage, quietly shutting the door behind him. Outside, he placed the rushlight on the windowsill, then slinked onto the rocky road, head on a swivel. As his eyes adjusted to the darkness, two shadows shifted closer, until John saw dim light reflecting from two pairs of eyes.

Something growled. "Ah, a ... morsel," John heard.

"Eat," said a second voice.

John drew an arrow back as the two figures lunged forward. The eyes bounded forward in time with the shadows' strides. Up, down, up, and one eye winked out forever. The figure tumbled to the ground. He didn't have time to nock another arrow before the second figure reached him. It slammed into his chest, knocking him to the ground. A drooling maw snapped at his throat, but John threw his arm up, and the teeth clamped down on his forearm.

Anger, usually buried deep within him, boiled to the surface. He rolled to the side so he was on top of the creature and thrust his forearm deeper into the creature's mouth while drawing his knife. The creature bit down.

John's arm sounded like a stick breaking.

John plunged the knife into the thing's neck over and over, as the creature tried to disengage. Its claws raked his chest. But the creature's mouth was full, and John had its head pinned in place. Eventually, the jaw relaxed and the creature shuddered. With a scream, John yanked his arm out of the thing's mouth, skin ripping on the sharp teeth. He stumbled toward his cottage, his vision growing blurry and blood dripping from his chest and arm. He made it a handful of steps before his legs crumpled.

John woke on the ground, blinking away pain, staring up at the night sky. Grunting, he struggled to sit. His left arm couldn't hold his weight, so he held it up. It looked wrong. Crooked. That's not right, he thought. He grabbed the wrist with his good arm and tugged. The world went black again.

⌣

He woke up on the ground again, blinking away the blackness at the edges of his vision. Anderson hovered into view with a tired smile and piercing blue eyes.

"Hey." John tried to stand but Anderson used a foot to gently push him back into the nest of blankets on the floor.

"Is she all right?" John asked, glancing at the bed.

"What? Yes, she's … fine. What happened to you?"

"I think I broke my arm." John winced while trying to sit up again. Anderson raised his eyebrow, and John lay down with a defeated sigh.

"Yes, I figured that out. Did you try setting it yourself? You are also covered in cuts. Somehow, you avoided puncturing any arteries, but you may need stitches, and …"

John interrupted. "What's an artery?"

"Blood tube. What happened?"

"Ah, I think that whatever cut her up came back for seconds," John said, shrugging. "What are you doing here anyway?"

"I came to pick her up, remember? Please explain to me what happened"

John rubbed his chin. "Um, I was attacked?"

"Yes, I gathered that." Sarcasm dripped from Anderson's voice. "You've got bites and scratches all over you, plus the burned bodies outside gave that away."

"Burned bodies?"

Anderson stared at John for a second.

"Ah fuck." Anderson looked out into the small clearing next to John's cabin.

John made it to his knees. "Help me up," he demanded. Anderson gave in.

Outside, looking down at the dog-shaped skeleton, John grunted. "Huh." Small pieces of burned flesh clung to the charred black remains. One empty eye socket stared up into the sky. Around them, the wind stirred ash. "That's just weird."

"Maybe," Anderson replied as John wandered over to the second blackened skeleton. He picked up its wolf-like skull.

"Maybe it's best if you don't touch ... stop using your arm!" Anderson exclaimed, exasperated. The arrowhead fell out through the mouth, clattering against the stone. John grunted in pain as he bent to pick it up.

"You really should be lying down, you know." Anderson rubbed the bridge of his nose.

"Shit," John said, examining the arrowhead. "It's just scrap metal now."

Anderson leaned forward for a better look. "You can't reuse it?"

"Nah, heat changes the, uh crystals inside. It needs to be retempered."

Anderson blinked. "How do you know that but don't know what an artery is?"

"Steel is useful." John shrugged. "I knew what an artery was. I just didn't know the name."

Anderson rolled his eyes. "Arteries and veins are both blood tubes. Arteries are connected to your heart, so they bleed more if they're cut."

John nodded. "I see."

"There's a third one over there." Anderson pointed. John wandered over to find another skeleton, head smashed in with a hoof-like imprint.

"Warhorse. Right." John smirked. He nodded to the white horse in thanks, but it was too busy eyeing the horse harnessed to Anderson's cart.

"It's not normal, you know," Anderson said. "The horse, I mean. And the rest of it," he added after a moment.

John grinned. "Yeah, this is pretty fucking weird."

Placing a hand on each side of John's face, Anderson studied his eyes. "Aren't you in pain?"

"Yeah."

"Well ... let's go back inside."

"You know what those are?" John asked, easing himself to the floor and motioning Anderson toward the only chair.

Anderson opened his mouth to say something, gave a dramatic sigh, and sat down. "So they aren't ..." Anderson began.

"They aren't Twisted, no," John said. "I know what Twisted look like."

Anderson grunted. "I heard stories before. I think they are nightmares."

"Nightmares?" John scratched at his cheek.

"Yeah, pulled from someone's sleep. They burn in the sun."

"Pulled from someone's sleep?"

"That's all I heard."

"Huh," was all John could say. "Someone had nightmares about wolves."

Anderson showed his palms. "It could be something else. I don't know much about this sort of thing. I mean, we are quite a distance from the Spire, and I am pretty sure these aren't church sanctioned, so ..."

"Yeah," John said. They lapsed into silence again. John glanced at the woman. "How is she doing?"

Anderson shrugged. "Her stomach wounds are deep. Her intestines are punctured, and she has a fever. Chances are that some of her shit is leaking into her blood."

John grimaced. "That's not good."

"No, it's not."

John suddenly stood up, staggering as he moved. Anderson stood to help, but John waved him off and headed to his lockbox. He unlocked it, eyeing its contents. A few coins, a small gem, and a silver spoon. Those were his. The rest—bracelets, rings, necklace—were hers. He held up the necklace. Dried blood stained the silver, but the eyeball-sized gem glistened. It seemed almost otherworldly. He held it up to his eye, and the room beyond morphed and rippled, like the gem contained swirling water. He handed the necklace to Anderson, who examined it with a furrowed brow while John scratched at the bandages on his chest.

"Weird shit." Anderson handed it back.

"Think it's a Storm gem?"

"Maybe," Anderson replied. "Certainly bizarre enough."

"It is a particular, indeed," said a musical voice. The woman pushed herself up in bed, smiling wryly at the two shocked faces.

Anderson rushed forward. "Listen, you have serious injuries. You need to lie back down."

She gave a short laugh, slapping his hand away. "I have lived plenty long enough, thank you very much. You. Hunter. Let me look at you. Yes." Suddenly, she looked ancient, but the moment passed. "Well then. I suppose … Yes, why not." She giggled to herself.

14

She pointed at John. "I name you my heir." Then she pointed at Anderson. "And you as my witness. I suppose that should be good enough, yes?" she said with a smile. Anderson opened his mouth to say something, but she cut him off.

"Keep the gem on you at all times. Don't trust anyone. Well, except for Cecil, but he's an idiot. Oh, I suppose I should feel a little guilty for this mess I am dropping on you but … I don't. Good luck."

She slumped, and Anderson helped her lie back down. Then she giggled again. "Do me a favor. When you see Trey, tell him to go fuck himself, will you?" Her head hit the pillow, and her eyes closed.

A moment passed in silence.

"Ma'am?" John asked.

Anderson felt the woman's neck. "I don't feel a pulse." He pressed his ear into her chest. "I think she's dead."

John stared at him, wide-eyed, blood-red gem still clutched in his hand.

"She named me as her heir?" John asked. "An heir for what?"

Anderson shrugged.

# 2

"Are you going to just ignore me the entire time?" Anderson sat at the front of the cart. Sprawled in the bed of the cart, John glumly watched the passing scenery. The white horse trotted along behind, placid.

The silence stretched out. Then Anderson turned to face him. "I know. I know. Sorry, as a doctor I have to insist."

"I hate it," John grumbled.

"I know. Only for a few days. Then you can go back to your cabin."

"They're going to bother me," John said. "They always do."

"I'll handle them," Anderson said. "You need to rest. Anyone being too nosy I'll put to work figuring out whoever she is." Anderson gestured at the blanket-wrapped figure next to John.

"Do dying people declare strangers their heirs often?" John asked.

"I don't think it's legally binding." Anderson paused. "Unless you signed something."

"No," John insisted.

"You did, didn't you?" Anderson gasped, his eyes twinkling.

"I didn't sign ..." John began, then saw Anderson's lips creep into a grin.

"Asshole," John grunted. But he smiled, and Anderson burst out laughing.

The cart continued to roll down the road, and Anderson suggested, "You should sleep."

John nodded and lay back on his blankets.

The dream was a strange one. Scores of vague shapes in black fog lined up in front of him. All were yelling, all wanting something, and all demanding to be let through. Behind him, John saw himself sleeping in the bed, a light shining from his chest.

One vague shape stepped up, a strong aroma of incense wafting around him. "I am a holy man!" it insisted.

John held up his hand. "Then give me wisdom." The shadow held up stone tablets, but the words slid off and the stones became blank. With a screech, the holy man stepped back into the fog, the incense fading with him.

A second stepped forward, claiming to be a merchant. John held up his hand. "Let me see your wares."

The shadow held up a bag. "Wonders beyond comprehension!"

John asked one more question. "What price did you pay for your wares?"

"A fair price!" the shadow insisted, but lies spilled from its eyes and nose. The fog swallowed the merchant.

A third stepped forward. "I am a nobleman."

John held up his hand. "Then tell me your vows." From its mouth tumbled many scrolls covered in strange letters. John picked up one. "Repeat what this says." The shadow yelled in frustration, then fell backward into the fog.

John woke with a pounding headache.

"Morning." Anderson's voice came from beside him. John looked up, blinking. He was in a bed, and Anderson sat on a chair at his side.

"How long was I out?" John sat up, plucking at bandages. He fingered the necklace around his neck and held up the red stone, giving Anderson a look.

"Ah, just in case. You were out for a day. You obviously needed the rest." He laid a hand on John's chest. "Please."

"Please what?" John growled.

"Please lie down. You had three horrible creatures try to eat you. And don't pick at your bandages."

John gave in. "How is everything?"

"A little chaotic. Everyone is grabbing pitchforks and patrolling the woods. So far there has been nothing."

John grunted. "They asking about me?"

Anderson made a face. "Yeah, they have been. I haven't said anything. Still no idea who the woman is. It's a big mystery. The horse is drawing attention as well. It's refusing to go into my stable. It's just standing in the marketplace near my door."

John laughed. "I bet that's freaking everyone out."

"It almost broke Ben's arm. It seems rather keen on staying near you." As if on cue, a shadow broke across the window, and the large head of a snowy steed poked into the room.

"Hey, horse," John said. It whinnied, then withdrew.

"Well, I guess it broke the tether ... again," Anderson said. But John, asleep once more, didn't hear.

⟿

John dreamed again. Another group of shadowy figures shouted from the fog, muted obscenities in unknown languages. Again, his body lay behind on the bed.

A man stepped out of the mist, every inch covered in glittering scrolls. His face was paper, forming the words, "Please let me through."

John asked, "What is your name?" The papers shimmered in bright ink spelling thousands of titles and honorifics across the man's body. "What is your name?" John repeated. The man snatched at the paper over his face, black ink dripped over his arms. Then the man fled back into the fog with a muffled scream.

Another figure stepped forward, a mere shadow with two eyes and a smiling mouth, all teeth. John raised his hand. "Show me your sense of self." The creature gestured and images of fantastic figures, each more noble than the last, appeared between them. John asked again, "Who are you?" The shadow screamed and was dragged back into the fog.

The third figure stepped forward, a shining suit of armor holding a whiskey bottle. Tears streamed from the visor, dripping to the ground. John asked him, "Why are you here?"

A voice in the armor said simply, "Duty and love."

John stepped aside, and the man strode past, toward John's sleeping form.

⟿

"John!" John woke with a start at the panic in Anderson's voice.

Someone else was in the room with them.

The man was clean-shaven, wearing a sky-blue shirt, brown pants, and a sword at his waist. He wore well-fitted gloves and a feather in his hat. He appeared handsome, refined, and noble—and obviously drunk.

He swayed before John's bed. John looked to Anderson, who seemed bewildered.

"How did you ... get here?" Anderson finally asked.

"Excuse me, sir.... May I?" The man pointed at the gem around John's neck. Wordlessly, John removed it and held it out. The man grabbed it. As he stared at his hand, the gem glowed.

Looking back at John, he breathed, "You're the heir."

John shook his head. "No."

"Sir, you must excuse me—" The man's voice trembled, and he pointed at John with his free hand. "—but you are the fucking *heir*." His hand holding the gem shook.

John denied the accusation more emphatically this time. "No, no, no."

The man paced, muttering, "Why? Why! What the hell was she thinking? You ... No, she's dead now. Dead." He stopped and looked at John again. "So you aren't *just* the heir anymore. Who are you?"

Behind him, Elizabeth peeked around the doorway, mouthing questions at Anderson. "Okay, just take the ..." John began, but the man threw the gem, hitting him in the chest. John winced.

"Sir, you are a gatekeeper now! The gatekeeper!"

"I don't know what a gatekeeper is," John stated.

The man stopped, staring slack-jawed. "You don't know anything? You don't know ANYTHING! Why are you the gatekeeper?" He stepped closer, fuming.

John held up the stone again. "Just take it. Please. I don't want to be part of whatever …"

The man screamed in frustration and punched the stone wall. "You cannot hand your gatestone out! Do you know what can happen to you if you do? You have to keep it on you! Excuse me, sir, but you are a complete, fucking moron!"

He panted for a moment, then took in John and Anderson's frightened expressions. He slurred, "You … you really don't know anything. My apologies. I am sorry, I was out of line. My apologies."

With that, he disappeared.

One moment he was standing there, and the next he was gone. No flash of light, no sound, just a slight breeze, barely enough to rustle a paper, and a lingering smell of cologne. A knock on the front door broke the silence.

"Hey, Anderson, we heard yelling. Is everything okay?" A voice spoke from the front of the house.

Anderson glanced at Elizabeth, who nodded. "I'll deal with it."

While John and Anderson sat in silence staring at where the man had been, they heard Elizabeth's muted conversation on the other side of the door: nightmare, fever-dream, strange man.

When she returned, Anderson finally spoke. "There is something going on. Something involved with Storm."

John buried his face in his hands.

"Well, this is certainly odd."

John stared up at the ceiling as Anderson examined his chest.

Anderson went on. "These wounds look at least a week old, not just a couple of days, the way they have healed."

"Fuck," John mumbled, then held up his arm. "Then can we take this off?"

Anderson removed the splint and examined his arm. "As a medical professional, it is my opinion that you should figure out how to get rid of that gem as soon as possible. It is probably full to the brim with Storm."

John did not reply.

"Listen," Anderson continued, "that man said not to let anyone else have it, and despite everything, I believe he was trying to help."

"Yeah."

"So, figuring out what to do with that thing should be your next priority. You should head to the city. Bring the body and the horse, of course. So far it's wrecked three gardens, so the townsfolk would appreciate it. They are terrified of it."

John nodded.

"I can put together provisions if you want. I have some friends there, if you want me to write you a letter."

"I ... know someone there." John continued staring at the ceiling.

Anderson looked down at John.

"John, I'm sorry. I know—"

"Stop," John said flatly. "I'll figure it out."

"Yeah. All right," Anderson replied. "Sleep on it, I'll get some things ready." Anderson patted him on the shoulder, then left him in silence.

⌣

The dreamscape changed again. This time, it was silent. A procession approached. At its head, a ghostly sprite flitted back and forth.

John held up his hand as they approached, and they stopped. The sprite hovered in front of his face.

"Hey, Dweeb, let me through."

"Why are you here?" asked John.

"Dad told me to," the sprite replied. John hesitated, and the sprite zipped past.

Next, a large, shielded man entered the procession. John could not see the mans face in the helm, but the eyes on the shield blinked in his direction. John waited.

"I am here to make sure she doesn't get herself killed," the figure said. John let him through.

The next one....

⌣

"Morning!" A peppy voice woke John. He stared at the woman standing over his bed. She looked like she was from the Great Delta with her black hair and smooth skin covering the corners of her eyes. Short and cute, she wore a lacy black dress with a red underdress, which gave her the appearance of smoldering coals. In her hand she held a chain which seemed to fade off into nothingness.

Behind her, a massive man in full plate armor stood, slouching to avoid hitting his head on the ceiling. John heard Anderson yelling in the next room.

"Um," John managed, staring at the odd chain in her hand, before being interrupted again.

"So, you're the new gatekeeper, huh? That's fun. You really should learn to open up a bit more."

"What?" John asked. Anderson stood in the doorway, staring at the giant man.

"There is a group of pallbearers in the kitchen," Anderson said, matter of factly.

The woman smiled at him. "Yep! We are here to pick up Husniye!"

"Who?" Anderson asked, paused, then said, "Yeah, all right. She's uh, in the temple."

Elizabeth sidled into the room. "What's going on?" she whispered to Anderson."

"Mages," Anderson mouthed.

Elizabeth nodded, the color draining from her face. She held out a basket to the strangers. "Do you want a muffin?"

The woman clapped her hands together. "A muffin would be excellent! Thank you!" She grabbed one and stuffed it into her mouth.

The giant armored man held up a hand, pleading. "Li. Please." His voice boomed. "Manners."

"Ish fine," Li said, with a mouthful of muffin.

Anderson and Elizabeth exchanged glances.

"Excuse me, so where is the body?" a pallbearer behind Anderson asked. Anderson turned and stared at the procession. Each wore black robes with red veils over their faces. Anderson paused, then gestured to the front door.

"Thank you, sir," the man said and silently shuffled past. The three behind him wrestled a wicker casket.

"Apologies," the lead bearer said, bowing at the giant man who shuffled to the side.

Li giggled and jumped on one of the empty beds and stood there grinning. The giant armored knight scowled at her.

"If you are going to stand on the bed, take your shoes off," he ordered.

Li made a face at him, rattling the chain around.

"A little to the left," one of the pallbearers whispered as they tried to maneuver the casket through the doorway.

"After you're through the door, go straight ahead. It's the temple in the town," Anderson said.

"Thank you, sir," the cloaked man said again. They slipped out into the morning light, the sound of birds singing and confused townsfolk yelling echoed through the air.

"Well," Li said, stepping off the bed. "My name's Li. I am from House Wu. I'm here to fetch you!" she said.

John stared at her. "Fetch me for what?"

"I am here to fetch the newest gatekeeper of the Council of the Rose! Of course, I am from the Council of the Dragon, but you weren't exactly letting anyone with an agenda through, were you?" Li smiled. A shadow in the doorway distracted them.

"Hey, Anderson...." The man trailed off, staring at the giant armored figure standing in the clinic. Anderson moved toward him.

"Listen, Davidson, things are getting a little weird." Anderson guided him away from the doorway.

Li turned back to John. "Anyway, since you weren't letting anyone through, they sent me."

John cupped the back of his neck. "What do you mean, not letting anyone through?"

Li stared at John for a moment. A massive grin spread across her face. "You don't know anything! Okay, yeah, okay, okay, right!" Her face flitted between surprise, exuberance, and confusion, before settling on exuberance. "So, as the contracted gatekeeper, you are the one who decides who is let through the gate. Of course, normally there is more than one gatekeeper per stone, but your stone is unusual. Anyway, you shouldn't be able to block people subconsciously, but who knows what Husniye did to the stone, so I suppose that's fair. Right? Anyway, it's freaking everyone out."

"The dreams," John said in the pause. Li stared at him, tilting her head and furrowing her brow as she processed his words.

"What contract?" John continued. Li clapped her hands.

"Well, Husniye made you the heir for the gatestone, which is a pretty big deal since that's the smallest gatestone in, you know, the entire Council of the Rose. But that makes you part of the contract with the Spire, right?" Li continued "And since you are in contract with the Spire, who subcontracts out to the Council of the Rose, sort of, to run the gatestones," she finished.

John looked at her, mouth open.

"Anyway, it's a whole thing. Basically, you have to follow the rules. But since they couldn't contact you, it was a mass panic, which is why I am here! They asked Wu for a favor, to see if I could get through to you. Plus, I know how to use the Chained Stone, so that's a plus." Li rattled the chain. John glanced at the strange links. The farther from her hand it got, the more transparent it got, until it was barely visible.

"Okay, so what are the rules?" John asked after a moment.

Li clapped her hands together, just in time for a commotion to start outside. "Oh geez, we should deal with that." Li nodded at the armored figure, who stepped outside.

The commotion increased tenfold.

"Let's go!" Li said. She grabbed John and attempted to drag him out of the bed.

John stood, still puzzled. "What's a gatestone?"

Li stopped and stared at him, then burst out laughing. "It's a teleporter! We use the gate for trade and moving soldiers and shit."

"Ah," John replied and followed her outside. "A red gate. I knew that. Right."

An angry, yelling mob surrounded the pallbearers. "You can't just claim her jewelry like that! We need paperwork!" someone screamed at a pallbearer, right before the man in armor picked him up and threw him back toward the crowd. After that, everyone decided to keep their distance.

"You have it all?" Li asked the lead pallbearer.

The man nodded.

"Good! Let's get out of this dump!" Li said, still holding the chain.

John held up a hand. "Wait a moment!"

"John! Your things!" Anderson tossed him a bag.

John caught it, catching Anderson's eye. "I am going to go deal with this."

"Good luck," Anderson said.

"Okay, let's g—" John's body suddenly felt like it had tipped sideways over a massive cliff to then freefall. Everything around him was a deep shade of purple, and shadows flitted around him. The chain was still in sight and seemed to go on for miles, to what looked like a mountain made of red crystal in the distance.

And as suddenly as the experience began, it ended.

# 3

John's ears rang. The sounds around him were muffled, and he struggled to bring a vaulted ceiling into focus. The ceiling, a work of art, displayed a painting of a massive serpentine figure breathing fire at armored figures waving yellow flags. As he waited for the world to stop spinning, John took several deep breaths. The tiled floor was cold against his back.

Li's face appeared above him. "Hey, you alive?"

He nodded.

She held out a bucket. "If you need to throw up. No shame in it."

John sat up, waving Li off. "I'm fine." He noticed the pallbearers on one side, and a crowd of important-looking people staring at him on the other. John lay back down. Li kicked him gently. "Up."

John grunted and stood, hefting his bag onto his shoulders. Wealth shimmered in the light of the mage lamps—light emitting crystals created by mages—and the jewelry of the onlookers sparkled unnaturally. To his left, a massive red crystal glowed. A system of iron rings and chains anchored it to the floor, as though the whole crystal might float away without them. With the appearance of liquid, the crystal's surface was constantly flowing and distorting. John felt queasy after a few seconds of looking at it.

A grinning man sauntered forward, arms outspread, as if he might embrace John. He wore a blue tunic with gold trim and contrasting black pants with a purple stripe down the side. A small hat with a feather topped his head, and his smile appeared practiced. "Welcome to Spire Island! The center of the world, and source of all magic. On behalf of the Spire, I welcome you as a new member of the Council of the Rose and wielder of a gatestone. Congratulations!" He doffed his hat with a bow and a flourish. The pallbearers solemnly marched away through the crowd, carrying the wicker casket.

"Who's the Rose Council?" John asked.

The man's face twitched, then composed itself. This time, he spoke as though addressing a child. "The Rose Council is a group of houses with responsibility for many of the Spire's gatestones."

John's memories of the world he had left years before began to stir. "Are you talking about House Romanov?"

"House Romanov is indeed a member of the Council of the Rose, sir. Now, why don't we—"

"I thought they owned the red gates wholesale?" John interrupted.

Now the man looked cross. "The gatestones—" The man emphasized the word. "—are owned by the houses, but the councils regulate travel between them."

John nodded "So how do I get rid of this?" He held up the gemstone around his neck.

"I'm sorry?" the man said.

"I don't want to get involved in any of this." John waved at the grandeur around him. "I just want to get rid of this and go back home."

"Let me introduce you to your fellow gatekeepers." The man motioned for John to follow him as he moved toward the waiting group.

"Fellow gatekeepers?" John clenched his jaw. Then, with a resigned sigh, he stepped in front of a tall man with intense eyes and pale skin. He wore a dark blue shirt, a purple sash, and black pants. His sword and buttons gleamed silver.

"Hello, I am Jacques Maximilian DuFort the third, current member of the Council of the Rose representing House DuFort and our many gatestones." He gave John a small bow. "I welcome you to the council, and I hope we can work together."

"The third ..." John replied slowly, vaguely recollecting Husniye's last words. "That's Trey, right? Trey is three or third?" Jacques Maximillian DuFort's eyes narrowed. "Does anyone call you Trey?"

The man blinked and gave a tight smile. "I prefer Sir Maximillian, if you don't mind."

"Did Husniye call you Trey?"

"That was the ... nickname she used, yes." The man's voice was icy.

"I have a message from Husniye. Go fuck yourself."

⌒

"You can wait here to be picked up." A strange woman gestured to a chair.

John sat down. "Wait for what?"

31

She looked confused. "For your house to come pick you up." She waited a moment, as if expecting John to understand, then explained, "You are at House Wu."

John continued to stare.

A man nearby cleared his throat. "I can take it from here." He wore a red tunic and brown pants with leather shoes. His attempt at simple clothing failed, given his elegant shoes and spiderweave tunic. The sword at his waist looked well-worn.

"Of course, sir." The woman bowed and shuffled away.

"Hello, sir," the man said.

"You're that guy," John said.

The man winced. He knew what John meant. "I am extremely sorry about that. My name is Cecil Husniye. I volunteered to come pick you up."

"You're the idiot!" John excitedly pointed a finger at the man.

"I'm sorry?" Cecil said, backing away.

"She said I could trust you!" John said. "And that you are an idiot."

Cecil gave a sad laugh. "Baba said that, huh?"

"Baba?"

Cecil shook himself. "The Gatekeeper of Olumtahss, the High Matron Songul Husniye of House Husniye. Sitting councilwoman of the Council of the Rose."

"Ah," John said. "Olumtahss?"

"That." Cecil pointed to the stone around John's neck.

"Oh." His hand immediately flew to it.

"I never got your name?" said Cecil.

"John."

"John what?"

"Just John is fine."

Cecil nodded. "Very well. By the way—" He cleared his throat. "—as a favor, can you not mention what happened? You know the …"

"Sure."

"Well, I have to thank you then." Cecil sighed with relief. He leaned closer, whispering, "So, why did you let me through, and no one else?"

John tilted his head. "You had a good reason."

"The others didn't?" Cecil asked, eyebrow raised.

"No," John replied. They lapsed into silence.

After a moment, Cecil started again. "Well, I have to know. Did Husniye really tell you to tell Trey to go, as you said, fuck himself?"

"Yeah, she did. It was technically her dying wish…. Plus it got me out of there faster. I'm just a country bumpkin, after all. No need for all that pomp."

Cecil looked like he was trying not to smile. "Do you know who he is? He's the head of House DuFort."

"Is that important?"

"Very."

"Oh. Whoops." John shrugged.

"Shall we go?" Cecil gestured down the hall.

John looked down the hall with him. "Where are we going?"

"House Husniye would like to speak with you. Specifically, Ahmet of House Husniye."

John stood. "Ahmet Husniye?"

"Ah, no, he's not a Husniye, but he is part of House Husniye."

"Oh," John muttered. "And you are a Husniye? You don't look much like her." He looked at Cecil's pale skin as they walked.

"I was adopted."

"What does he want?"

"Well, quite a number of things," said Cecil.

"Like …?"

"Like you are a gatekeeper now."

John halted, planting his feet. "I am not a mage."

"What? Gatekeepers don't have to be mages."

John shook his head firmly. "Those fellows stand next to the red gates, putting their hands on them and muttering? Those are mages."

"Yes," Cecil admitted, "but gatekeepers don't always have to be mages."

"Are you a gatekeeper?" John asked, almost like an accusation.

"No, but Trey is. Most high-ranking nobles are, since their status affords them legal protection, even if they don't put the work in."

John continued to try and figure out what was what. "So they aren't real gatekeepers, then?"

"Legally, they are."

John glared, holding up the gem around his neck. "And this is a red gate."

"Yes, that's a gatestone. But they aren't always red."

"So now I am legally a gatekeeper," John said stoically. "And what does Ahmet want?"

"That stone is important to House Husniye. We wish to discuss your new situation and see if we can come to an amicable resolution. Which is politic speak for shit has hit the fan and now we need to figure everything out."

John gave a small laugh. "Lead the way, I guess."

They arrived at a heavy door. A robed man opened it and waved them in. "Right this way, sir."

Cecil addressed the man. "I and House Husniye would like to thank House Wu for letting us use their facilities." After a clink of coins, the man bowed and left, closing the door behind him.

The room was small, with chairs arranged in front of a large, flat green stone. Everything smelled like a mix of perfume and old cushions. Cecil placed his hand on the polished surface, muttering quietly.

John backed into a corner of the room as the stone started to glow. "Is that a talk stone?"

"Comm stone," Cecil corrected. "And seer stone." He stepped away and sat down, motioning for John to do the same.

John looked around the empty room. "For just the two of us?"

"What?"

"Aren't these expensive? Seems like a waste." John muttered as he sat down. The stone flickered, and a fuzzy shape appeared on it.

"Hello? Can you hear me?"

"Hello, Ahmet, this is Cecil. Can you see us?"

"I can see you perfectly! Ah, is that …"

"Yessir, that's the new gatekeeper."

"Wonderful, they were able to retrieve him! How are you doing, sir? It's a pleasure to finally meet you."

"You are blurry," John stated.

Cecil winced, then muttered to John, "Sorry, I'm not good at this."

"Apologies," Ahmet said, his image on the stone flickering. "You have been a hard man to contact. Is there a reason you were denying transport requests?"

John shrugged. "Nobody gave me a good reason to let them through."

"I see. ... Sir, I don't believe we've met before."

"We haven't," John agreed.

"Then may I ask your name?" The image seemed to lean forward to see him better.

"My name is John."

"John who?"

"Just John is fine."

"May I ask how you knew Husniye?"

"I didn't."

Even with the shifting image, John could see the concern on Ahmet's face. "But you are the new gatekeeper for Olumtahss, correct?"

"Olumtahss?" John hesitated. "Oh, yeah, this thing." He held up the gem.

"What do you do for a living, John?"

"I live in the woods."

Cecil stared at him, open-mouthed.

John went on. "This lady came to my home, declared me the heir, then died."

Ahmet gave a slight headshake. "What happened? How did she die?"

"From her wounds," John explained. "Monster attack of some sort."

Ahmet coughed. "Let me get this straight: she just showed up at your doorstep, wounded, declared you the heir, then died?"

John gave a little shrug. "Yeah, basically."

"Thank you, John," Ahmet said. "Cecil, may I talk to you in private for a moment?"

As John returned to his chair, Cecil stepped close to the stone and placed his hand on it. He whispered things to Ahmet for a few moments, then dropped his hand, and Ahmet's image vanished. Cecil turned and clapped his hands together. "Well, sir, there are a few people who want to meet you. We are going to have dinner at House Husniye."

"Do I have to?"

"Yes." Cecil looked him over. "And you will need new clothes."

John looked down at his stained shirt. "These aren't that bad." Seeing Cecil's face he went on, "Kidding. But I'm not paying for it."

"House Husniye will cover everything," Cecil promised. "Let's get moving."

⌒

The men walked down stone roads lined with towering houses, each with a different architectural style, creating a chaotic mosaic. Every twenty paces a massive stone column loomed with a mage light on top. Pedestrian traffic was light, yet carriages thronged the streets. Giant, four-legged creatures that appeared to be carved from stone drew some. Purple light could be seen through cracks in their bodies as they plodded down the road.

"We can get a carriage if you want," Cecil suggested, "though I would not mind walking."

John considered the stone monstrosity lumbering past. "Is that Storm?"

"Storm?" Cecil was surprised. "No, we say magic here. We consider "Storm" insulting. And I have found when dealing with mages, it's important to be respectful."

"So how do you stop people from being Twisted?"

"What?" Cecil laughed uncomfortably. "That's not really a thing."

"I've seen one," John said, flatly.

"Oh. Well." Cecil made steady eye contact with the ground. "Listen, it's not something you really want to bring up around here. But there are safeties in place."

"Safeties?"

"Rules and regulations!" Cecil said, suddenly chipper again. "Tons of rules, paperwork to fill out, that sort of thing."

"Do people follow these rules?" John asked.

"Of course!" Cecil replied, looking away.

"So how do the rules stop Twisted from forming?"

"If you use the right tool, there isn't any magic leakage," Cecil explained.

"Do people always use the right tool?"

"Yes, absolutely."

They stepped around a group of women, and one waved at Cecil. He waved back with a smile, which John saw him drop as soon as they were past.

"What tool do those use?" John pointed at another stone carriage monster.

"An ancient, powerful one. Well-tested over the years. Do you see the driver there?" Cecil nodded toward a mage, sitting cross-legged at the front of the carriage, who was staring intently at the creature. "He is sitting on a powerful spellcircle that controls and steers the golem. He's not actually a mage, despite appearances. Of course, he has some mage training."

"Ancient? Do they ever break?"

"They get inspected every three months." Cecil looked at John's face, clicked his tongue, then went on more gently. "Listen. See these symbols?" He pointed to an ornate metal pattern inset into the road every ten meters. "Those eat magic. Any leaks get dealt with quickly. Stay on the roads, and don't go into any alleyways, for a multitude of reasons. But the roads are very safe. Any Twisted get taken care of quickly."

"Thanks," John breathed.

"Also, try not to bring up Twisted with anyone else, ok? Bit of a taboo subject." Cecil stopped and pivoted. "This way."

John noticed a subtle change in the massive stone houses. Although each retained its wild style, they shared a similarity John couldn't put his finger on. One was blue stone with red roof tiles, the next, pitch black with a mirror-like sheen and a white roof that refracted rainbow light. Outside each, soldiers wearing purple and black stood at attention.

Suddenly, he saw the pattern. "The windows in all these houses are the same."

"Good eye. These are all from the western continent." Cecil waved at the black one with the white roof with his hand. "Agiamor. Knights of the Black Stone? I think that's how it's translated. Obsidian."

"I got that. Each house here is a different … group?" John asked.

"They are called houses for a reason. Like House Husniye."

"Why?"

"Well, this is an island, one of the few places where magic is practiced freely. The Spire manages it, of course." Cecil nodded at the massive tower, its tip peeking above the houses to their left. "They also run the gatestone network, so all the major nobility and merchant groups want representation here."

"So they built these?"

Cecil leaned in with a slight smirk and whispered, "It started as a dick-waving contest." Behind him, an exceptionally obese man on a palanquin was being paraded down the road, surrounded by standard bearers. Everyone ignored him.

"A what?" John asked.

"A dick-waving contest. What, you never compared sizes?"

"I never waved it around," John said. "Is that a thing?"

"Well, look around!" Cecil said, throwing up his arms. "Biggest one in the world. Of course, it's not that simple. There are uhh …" Cecil waved his hand, searching for the words. "Expected duties every house must perform? Taxes, basically."

"You buy into the club to get the benefits." John looked around. "And each house provides soldiers in exchange for access to the Spire?"

Cecil gave him a sidelong glance. "Yes, that's exactly right. Have you heard about it before?"

"No. It's just … the guards outside each house have the same uniform." John pointed. "But they all look different. Obviously provided by the house itself."

"Yes, purple and black is the color of the Spire. Every soldier provided to patrol the streets has to be in Spire uniform and enforce Spire law."

"They aren't patrolling," John noted.

"Spire law has to be enforced until you cross the gateway of the house. Plus, technically, the guards are keeping peace of this section of road." Quietly, he added, "They can use it as a tax write-off. Left here."

On the next road, John spotted a group of females dressed in a skirt uniform that displayed plentiful cleavage and skin. Led by a man in a black robe with a white mask, they all wore some kind of collar. The crowd parted before them, looking away.

"What's with that?"

"Don't worry about that," Cecil said quickly.

John stopped, and Cecil moved forward several paces before turning around. "John, please."

"What's with that?" John repeated, pointing at the scene.

Cecil grabbed his arm and lowered it. "Don't point, don't make eye contact."

"Is that a slaver?"

Cecil bit his lip. "Well, yes."

"They didn't even have the decency to put them in a covered cart?" John's voice rose as the group disappeared.

"They were trying to show them off. For buyers. They always do that.

"Really? Those collars ..." John shook his head.

Cecil gripped his arm. "Well, yes, but can we not have this conversation right now?"

John shook his hand off his arm. "We are having it now."

Cecil glanced around, then whispered. "They use magic to enslave the minds of people, okay? Do not anger them." Talking normally, Cecil continued. "Husniye doesn't get involved in that sort of thing, but if you haven't noticed, there are a lot of different people here, each with their own way of doing things. There are rules. One of the biggest is to mind your own business. So let's go."

John ran his fingers through his hair. "The church allows that?"

"The Storm Church? They have no power here." Cecil waved him forward and resumed walking.

John followed. "Don't call it the Storm Church. That's considered rude. They are the Church of the Clear Sky."

"Really?" Cecil looked genuinely perplexed. "They've always introduced themselves as the Storm Church."

John made a face. "Different sect, I suppose," he muttered. Cecil glanced at him sidelong, eyebrows furrowed, but he didn't press the issue.

They walked in silence as John took in the sights. Suddenly, a thought occurred to him, and he blurted, "After the tailor, are we walking to House Husniye?"

"Yes. Unless you want to take a carriage?"

"And Ahmet is there?"

"Yes."

"So we used a seer stone when we could have just walked over and talked to him?" John was aghast. And the lack of understanding on Cecil's face angered him. John waved his hands in agitation. "That's a massive waste! Seer stones are expensive! This is the problem with mages. You people play around with magic like it's nothing and then act surprised when Twisted run amok outside the walled zones!"

"I'm not a mage, John."

"You know what I mean!"

"You are on Spire Island. Maybe try and keep the Storm Church stuff to a minimum, okay?"

John threw up his hands. "Fine."

They walked the rest of the way to the tailors in silence.

"No, no, this won't do. Take off your shirt," demanded the short, dark-skinned man. A pin stuck out of the corner of his mouth and a tape draped around his neck. He wore a black robe, embossed with muted colors. Silently, John took off his stained shirt and let it drop to the ground.

"By the stones, what happened to you?" The man gaped at the dirty bandages and dried blood. Cecil's mouth dropped too.

"A monster tried to kill me," John said.

Cecil stared at John's chest. "A monster?"

"Yeah, I think it's one of the creatures that killed Husniye." One of the tailor's assistants gasped and ran from the room.

John furrowed his brow, remembering. "Anderson said they might be something called a nightmare?"

"A nightmare? A Storm drawn? A Summon?" Cecil asked.

"I don't know what those words mean."

"Why didn't you mention this before?" Cecil accused.

"Didn't really come up," John said.

Cecil turned to the tailor. "Do you have bath houses available?"

"Of course, sir. I'll arrange a bath and a quick medical checkup."

Cecil stepped close to John and murmured, "Keep an eye on the stone."

John nodded. Just before the door closed behind them, he saw Cecil collapse into a chair and cover his face with his hands.

⌐

Freshly clothed and smelling of citrus, John plodded sullenly alongside Cecil.

"So, this is it," Cecil said, stopping in front of a stone building with red accents. The building was small compared to the houses that towered on either side, but still larger than any structure in the village near John's home. In fact, adding all the buildings in the village together wouldn't equal the size of this construction.

Cecil nodded at the two uniformed guards outside as they passed through the door. A black-robed woman hustled up to them as they crossed the threshold. She hissed icily at Cecil. "You are late."

"Sorry, Ahu. We got held up with something. Where is Ahmet?"

"No time. You are going straight to the meet and greet."

Cecil winced, but Ahu motioned for them to follow. They hurried down the stone corridor, shoes rustling on the red carpet. At the end of the passage, Ahu pulled open a massive door with a grunt. She motioned John through. Cecil shot him a look of pity. "Good luck."

Squaring his shoulders, John stepped forward.

# 4

"Ah, John. A pleasure to meet you. My name is Ahmet." A corpulent man crossed the hall and extended a hand, which John shook while sizing him up.

He was supremely obese. Though he wore garments intended to minimize his girth, they failed. The enormous turban only added to his size. "So glad you could join us. Welcome to House Husniye. We are a small house, only managing around a dozen gatestones, but our passion makes up for it. I am currently acting as head of House Husniye. Let me introduce you to everyone."

John extracted his now sweaty hand from the man's grasp.

A second woman stepped forward and gave a small bow. "Hello, John. My name is Beyzra. It's a pleasure to meet you." She wore a simple brown robe, which accented her jewelry—a necklace and gold bracelets, both studded with glittering red opals. "I am so sorry for your loss. Husniye was a greatly esteemed woman," she said.

John furrowed his brows. "I didn't really know her."

"Um." Beyzra exchanged glances with Ahmet, eyes wide. "Then, if you don't mind me asking, how did you end up as gatekeeper of Olumtahss?"

"She collapsed in front of my house, then declared me her heir right before she died," John said.

There was a moment of silence while she seemed to gather her thoughts. "Well ..." the woman stuttered. "I suppose it's fortuitous that such an event let us meet."

"Sure," John said.

"Husniye founded this house, you know, using that gatestone. I remember the first time we met. I was a child still, just after my menarche. She rode into town from the wilderness, stone around her neck. We were not a large city, and we didn't have a gatestone of our own, you see. She let anyone in the town use Olumtahss for whatever they could offer her. She ended up with piles of fish and sacks of grain!" Beyzra smiled. "My father gave her a necklace, made from woven vines with a single red opal. You could find those all over in the nearby hills. Thanks to Husniye, exporting those opals became a big business for us, and eventually we were able to purchase a gatestone of our own. Many small towns' first experience with gatestones was Olumtahss. She was quite the philanthropist."

"She sounds like an amazing woman," John muttered.

She nodded. "Many of us here aspire to be like her. Well, except for the refusal to get married. That part was a scandal."

"Oh, mom." A young woman behind her muttered.

"Ah, I should introduce my daughter, Roshan." Beyzra gestured and the girl stepped forward. Unlike her mother, she wore a beautiful dress, accented with reds. A large opal on a gold chain rested on ample, exposed cleavage.

"An absolute pleasure to meet you," she said, bowing. John offered a slight wave, and another awkward moment of silence followed.

"Well, allow me to introduce Erik Rus," interrupted Ahmet. He waved over an older gentleman with a bushy white beard and eyebrows, eyes of piercing blue, and skin the color of aged maple wood. His appearance reminded John of Anderson, though his mannerisms were different.

The man stepped close, supported by a cane. "It is an honor to meet the next gatekeeper of Olumtahss. I handle ship trade within House Husniye."

"Ship trade?"

"Well, most of the time. Sometimes Husniye would ride along, and we anchored outside port and engaged in trade." Erik's eyes twinkled.

"Outside of port? Oh. You undercut the local merchants," John said with a glare, and Erik burst out laughing.

Ahmet stepped between them, took John's elbow, and turned him. "This is Alriyh, one of House Husniye's first members."

A tall, dark-skinned man, in simple yet high-quality clothing, strode forward. Beside him, Cecil rushed to keep up. John saw an angry flash in the man's eyes and stepped back as Alriyh stuck his face right in front of John's. "How did you end up as the gatekeeper? How did Husniye die?"

"Easy, Alriyh." Cecil held out a hand. "He's wounded. He fought off the Summon that killed Husniye. I saw the wounds myself," Cecil said.

Muttering broke out in the background.

Alriyh gave a heavy sigh and stepped back. "I apologize for my rudeness. Would you mind telling us the story of what happened?"

"I am afraid that we are already running late, and the dinner ..." Ahmet began.

Alriyh cut him off. "I want to hear what happened to Husniye."

"He can share the story after dinner," Ahmet argued, and Alriyh drew himself up, stepping toward Ahmet.

John blurted, "Here's the short version." The room fell silent as all eyes turned to him. "Uh, so Husniye showed up at my home with a serious stomach wound, and Anderson, he's the doctor, said shit had gotten into her blood."

"Sepsis," someone whispered.

"Anderson decided that we would move her in the morning...."

"So you decided to leave a woman to die because it would have been inconvenient?" Alriyh barked.

"Inconvenient?" John's own voice rose. "It was dark. We didn't have a stretcher, and it would have taken at least two days to take her to the city. Anderson had to get more supplies. I slept on the floor so she could have the bed." John stared Alriyh down. Through a clenched jaw, he growled, "It was a good thing we didn't move her either because the nightmares attacked that night."

"You mean Summons, right?" Erik Rus spoke up.

"Right," John said. "The creepy talking wolf-things." There was another spurt of whispering, and the word "talking" echoed throughout the room.

"Then what?" Ahmet asked.

"I killed them. Well, two of them. The horse killed the third."

"How?" Alriyh pressed.

"One with an arrow, one with a knife." When Alriyh grunted, John went on. "Then the next morning, when we were getting ready to move her, she woke up, declared me the heir, and then died," John said.

After a moment, Alriyh asked, "Who else was there?"

"Well, I live alone. But Anderson was there at the time."

Ahmet slapped John on the back like they were old friends. "Well, why don't we head to the main hall for dinner now?"

⌣

Stepping into the grand room, John sucked in a quick breath at its beauty. Brightly dyed fabric festooned the ceiling beams, making the room glow like a sunset. Mage lights cast a bright illumination over the room. Tables of an almost-black wood filled the space, lined with padded benches in a haphazard arrangement that struck John as odd. The people that filed in were as colorfully arrayed as the room. John was now openly staring at the many sights.

A mural covering one wall depicted a large skeletal hand holding what looked like the Olumtahss gatestone. Grains of sand filtered between the fingers and formed dunes. Men dressed like Alriyh trekked across them. A figure he recognized as Husniye stood among them, with Olumtahss around her neck, shining an iridescent red. Ships rode waves, women bedecked in red jewelry danced, and bearers held fine silks in baskets.

A black-robed man interrupted his thoughts, bowed toward John, and asked, "Your surname, sir?"

"Don't have one," John lied.

The man and Ahmet looked stunned. "Have you a clan then?"

John shook his head. "I'm a hermit."

"Um. Then what is your profession?"

"Hunting." They didn't need to know any more than that.

The man bowed again, stepped forward, and raised his arms. "Members and guests of House Husniye, I present to you, John Hunter the Hermit!"

Ahmet stood, arms out. "In our time of sorrow and the loss of our beloved leader, we have a glimmer of hope! Let me welcome John, the newest gatekeeper of House Husniye!"

As applause echoed around the room, John grumbled, "Gatekeeper of House Husniye."

Ahmet guided him to his chair with a firm grasp of his arm. Next to John was a brown-skinned man in a turban, wearing a blue robe and sporting a chest-length beard. He smiled at John as he sat down.

Four tables, arranged in a semicircle, faced John's table. He barely had time to take in the scene before Ahmet, standing next to him, spoke. "Once again, in our possession, we have the legendary gatestone, Olumtahss!" Ahmet gestured.

Next to John, the turbaned man muttered, "Take it out and show them." When John complied, the applause grew louder.

Ahmet held up his hands for silence. "The loss of Husniye was tragic. I do not believe we will ever have a replacement for her, nor would we try. She was truly unique, and her absence will be felt for years to come." Ahmet bowed his head. Everyone except for Alriyh bowed their heads as well. He hadn't moved since they'd entered the grand room, and he continued to glare at John.

"Yet we must move forward! As Husniye always said, 'Stagnation is the enemy of adaptation.' We must adapt! We must move forward to a new era of House Husniye!" The fat on his arms jiggled as he gestured wildly. Another round of polite applause.

As Ahmet sat next to John, a man stood at the table farthest to the right, his robes swirling among the myriad of silky clothing and glowing gems that shimmered around him in the room's light. "We of the Soissens Conglomerate are very sad to see Husniye leave this world. She was an amazing woman, an astute leader, and a fantastic business partner. We hope her parting will merely be the turning of the page of the story, leading to new chapters, opportunities, and profit." He returned to his seat.

Now Beyzra stood. The people at her table all sported darker clothing that made their brilliant red opal jewelry stand out even more. "Husniye was the light of this house, and without her, it feels very dark indeed. I considered her both a friend and a mentor. I hope we can keep her legacy alive."

As she sat, Erik stood. His table was a motley group of grizzle-bearded men. "When I was younger, if you told me I would be part of a Spire house, I would have laughed at you. Husniye truly was something special if she could domesticate me, even a little. I hope that the spirit of House Husniye, the little streak of wildness, never fades and we continue to persist for the ages."

Everyone looked toward Alriyh's table next. The people of the house were simply dressed, in tan robes with little jewelry. Alriyh spoke without standing. "Husniye was the glue that held this house together. She made the right choices, she handled the infighting, and she chose responsible heirs of good report. One of the heirs is dead, and the other is missing. So now we have this." Alriyh waved at John. "He is no replacement."

A shocked silence followed, and Ahmet shot to his feet, clapping his hands, "Well, let us eat!"

Lines of servants carrying trays burst through the doorways around the dining room, distributing dishes to claps of excitement. John watched as one plopped a massive bowl full of brown goop down next to him.

"Here, here, have some!" Ahmet ladled a few scoops, then grabbed John's spoon and stuck it in the bowl, like a conqueror claiming new land. John tried to smile back as he lifted the spoon, blew on it a few times, then gingerly placed it in his mouth. The taste exploded, creamy meat with unknown spices.

"What do you think?" Ahmet asked between mouthfuls. "It's one of our specialties, a meat curry."

"It tastes far better than it looks." John realized his mistake and stammered, "Not that.... I mean, it tastes great. Really. It just looks ..." He trailed off as Ahmet chuckled and slapped the table. John slumped and concentrated on spooning the curry into his mouth.

From the Soissens Conglomerate table, the man in swirling robes called out, "So, what is the current status of the Wetstone Conglomerate membership application?"

Ahmet carefully put his spoon down and wiped his mouth. "We are still waiting for the bureaucracy to catch up, unfortunately. I'll let you know as soon as the paperwork goes through."

Beyzra piped up next. "What about our network expansion regarding Agiamor? Have ... recent events ... delayed it?"

"There shouldn't be any delay with that," Ahmet replied.

John ate in silence, watching it all play out. Their conversation felt more like an interrogation than a friendly meeting, as everyone peppered Ahmet with question after question. The turbaned man next to John startled him out of his reverie.

"We haven't met yet. My name is al-Haytham. I'm the librarian, and I also moonlight as the head mage. Pleased to meet you, John."

"Likewise," John said once he had swallowed. "What did he mean by the 'heirs are missing or dead'?" John whispered. Al-Haytham winced.

"What Alriyh said? The heir Husniye had chosen before you met with an unfortunate accident. And her second choice went missing."

"And now I'm the heir."

Al-Haytham raised an eyebrow. "You are a bit more than an heir, at this point."

"Right," John muttered. Other questions distracted al-Haytham, so John let his eyes wander. He spotted Cecil at the back of the room standing at attention, dressed in a blazing-red shirt with white pants and a turban. Others, at the fringes, dressed in similar garb. Must be House Husniye's military dress uniform, John thought.

As John finished his curry, Alriyh spoke up again, voice cracking around the room. "Any progress in finding Ece?"

Ahmet cleared his throat. "I have contacted everyone I can, and I have agents scouring for any hints." He raised his hand before Alriyh could continue. "This isn't the first time she has disappeared like this. She may not even know Husniye has passed, and I am sure the second she finds out she will hurry back."

Alriyh slammed the table with his fist. "We should be kicking down doors looking for her."

"We cannot afford to make any enemies."

Alriyh rose and bellowed, "You know who has her!"

"We have no evidence!" Ahmet yelled back. "We cannot afford to make any baseless accusations at this time. We are in a very precarious position."

Alriyh walked around the table toward Ahmet, but Cecil placed a hand on his shoulder, whispering something. Alriyh brushed Cecil off, then stormed out of the room. The rest of his table also stood and left, some bowing politely before leaving.

The head of the Soissens Conglomerate's table spoke up, just loud enough for everyone to hear, but quiet enough that everyone could pretend they didn't. "I guess now we can have a civilized discussion." He signaled at the now empty table.

John watched al-Haytham wince. "Andrew, you absolute buffoon," he muttered. The mood in the room grew icy, and John suddenly found the mural behind him extremely interesting.

"Interested in our history?" Ahmet asked, loudly. Startled, John twitched and looked at Ahmet, who was already standing and gesturing eagerly at the mural.

"It started with one of Husniye's adventures. Her wanders took her into the desert, where she dueled an ancient wizard, taking his soulstone." Ahmet pointed at the image of Olumtahss in the skeletal hand. "She used it to create Olumtahss, and started her personal trade network, meeting with local merchants and connecting them to the main gatestone network. She traveled from town to town, acting as a temporary gate. This was the founding of House Husniye," Ahmet said. He pointed at the image of a woman carrying silks and other fine goods in baskets. "Beyzra was one of the first merchants to join up with Husniye, selling opals to the wider world.

"Later, she met up with our good man Erik here, and they began to expand." Ahmet pointed at a sailing ship. "She purchased her first solid gatestone for Beyzra." Ahmet pointed to the painting of a giant red stone. "And began expansion. Eventually, this led her to found House Husniye proper, licensed by the Spire." Ahmet moved to the last painting in the mural, a painting of the building they were in now. Ahmet turned back to John, waiting for a response.

"That's ... fascinating," John managed to say. Ahmet laughed, patted him on the back, and sat back down.

With that, the dinner ended, and Cecil escorted John back to his room.

⌒

Cecil turned down the mage lights at night, giving the hallway an eerie pall. Back in his room, John exclaimed, "Oh, my bag is here." Glancing at the furniture, he commented, "You know, the room at House Wu was grander."

"I apologize. They put you in one of the rooms for visiting foreign dignitaries. Do you want a bigger room?"

"No." John shook his head. "I was just curious."

Cecil prepared to leave. "I hope you have a good night's sleep. Your baths are in the side room there." Cecil nodded at a door. "I will see you tomorrow."

"What happened to the heir before me?" John asked.

"Maria? She was poisoned." He then rubbed a hand over his face. "I mean, she just fell ill. There isn't any proof of wrongdoing, just rumors."

"Who poisoned her?"

"It's just a rumor. But, if it is true, then Trey would have been the culprit."

"Why would Trey poison her?"

"Again, it's just a rumor. There is no evidence, but he did have a motivation. Their prenup agreement made Trey the heir if something were to happen to her."

"Prenup? They were married?"

"He can be very charming when he wants to. Maria fell for him and thought it would be a good political alliance. Husniye was against it."

John's heart thumped. "So if Husniye died before making me the heir, Trey would have gotten the stone."

Cecil nodded.

John stared at the floor, eyebrows furrowed, absorbing this information. "One more question."

"Go ahead."

"Who is Alriyh?"

"One of Husniye's oldest allies. His grandfather and Husniye fought the wizard whose soulstone they used to create Olumtahss."

"Grandfather? How old was Husniye?"

"She never said," Cecil said with a pained smile. John nodded.

"I'll see you tomorrow." Cecil closed the door, leaving John alone with his many thoughts.

# 5

John was already awake when a knock sounded on his door. He slid out of bed, trying to tame the bedhead he woke up with. Outside the door stood Cecil, and next to him, a woman held some clothes.

Cecil gave a small bow. "Good morning, John. I hope you slept well. You have a bit of a day ahead of you. This is Ahu, she'll help you prepare." The woman stood with her hands together as John blinked sleepily at them both.

"So you want me to strip in front of you?" he blurted.

Ahu frowned. "No, in the washroom. Before your bath."

"I had a bath yesterday."

"And you'll have another." Ahu dropped the clothes on a table and motioned John to follow her. "I'll show you how to use it."

After a brief tutorial on how to use the bath, and a promise that he did not in fact need help getting dressed, John was soon clean and ready.

Cecil shot him a grin. "Looking good."

"Thanks?"

As Ahu began to tidy the room behind him, Cecil explained, "So, the plan today is to have a late breakfast with Ahmet and the other heads of the house. After that, nobody could agree on anything, so we'll have to see where it goes." Cecil looked tired. "I suspect you aren't going to have much chance to eat, so if you want, we can head to the kitchen for some food now."

"That sounds great. Lead the way."

They walked the hallways in silence. Erik Rus suddenly stepped from around a corner. "Ah, John! And Cecil! Getting an early start, I see. Mind if I talk to John for a moment?"

"He's right here." John's gaze flitted between the two men, eyebrows furrowed.

Erik smirked. "I just wanted to know … are you a wildman?"

From the corner of his eye, John saw Cecil wince.

John said, "No."

"But you live outside the walls."

"Well, yes. But I live in nullstone fields. No need for walls, the Twisted stay away."

"Ahh." Rus breathed. "It's interesting that nobody ever wants to say they are wildmen. Whenever I ask, the answer is always no. Sure, we live outside the walls, in the wild, but we aren't those crazy lunatics you read about in stories. It's those other guys, obviously." He grinned slyly at John. "Many of the founders of this house came from outside the walls, me included. That was Husniye's style. People like saying that nothing exists outside the walls except for Twisted, Storms, and Abominations, but that's hardly true, is it?" Erik affixed John with a stare, which John met. Cecil looked like someone was standing on his foot.

When John did not reply, Erik went on. "My point is, in most houses, you would have no prospect of membership. Here, though, things are different." He paused again. When John didn't take the bait, he continued. "Our house bylaws declare the gatekeeper of that gatestone," he gestured toward the stone around John's neck, "to be the head of the house."

"What?" John stepped back.

Cecil rushed forward, a hand upheld. "Since he is not a member of the house, we decided he couldn't be the head of the house."

"Of course. I just wanted to make sure he knew his position." Erik turned from Cecil to meet John's eyes. "And, that if he ever needed anything, I'm available. Don't be a stranger now. I'll see you at the brunch." He sauntered away.

As his footsteps faded away, Cecil turned to John. "Let's hurry before anyone else shows up."

"Is that true?" John hurried to match Cecil's pace.

"Yeah, it is."

"Huh."

They slipped into the kitchen through the side door. A whir of activity greeted them: knives on cutting boards and the aroma of garlic, frying onions, and grilled meat permeating the room. Cecil led John to a small table, where the earliest rising staff were eating. One looked up and waved.

"Hey, captain!"

"Captain?" John glanced over.

Cecil gave a dismissive gesture and addressed them. "Hey, fellows, I was wondering if we could slip in a quick, quiet breakfast."

"Course! We'll rustle that up for you. Who's that?" the staff member said, pointing at John.

"Friend of mine." Cecil turned to John. "Have a seat, I'll grab you a bowl." Soon, he returned with a tray.

"So, Cecil, any news about Ece?" someone spoke up. Cecil paused, spoon halfway to his mouth, and shook his head. "Nothing yet. Not even a whisper."

"If they can't find her—" a man across from them began.

Cecil cut him off. "They will."

"But if they can't, who would be the next head? Ahmet?"

"We haven't decided yet."

"I hope it's not Ahmet," a woman farther down the table said. "He cares too much about money."

"What's wrong with that?" her neighbor asked.

"My hometown's gatestone isn't profitable."

Cecil chuckled. "Half the gatestones run by this house aren't profitable. Well, maybe more like a fourth."

"Then why run them?" John asked.

"Charity, basically. Without a gatestone, a lot of towns can become isolated, so having one is a big help."

John nodded. "Right, overland travel can be dangerous. Especially if a herd of Twisted is moving through the area."

"Exactly. Ahmet used to complain that Husniye was just using the house to pay for all these charity cases. And, well, there was some truth to it."

A sullen silence fell over the table.

"I can't believe she is really gone," another voice lamented.

They ate in silence for a few moments, before Cecil nudged John. "Want seconds?"

John spooned up the last few mouthfuls in his bowl and stood to follow Cecil.

⌒

"Ah, there he is!" Ahmet stood up surprisingly fast for someone his size and closed the distance between them in an instant, clapping John on the back in a friendly manner. "We were waiting for you." He gave Cecil a look of disdain.

This was a different space from last night's banquet hall, more like a lounge, with soft pillows scattered everywhere. Tables covered in food and drink lined the walls. "If you are hungry, help yourself!"

John drew close to the nearest table, overwhelmed by the array of strange food. He read a label out loud. "Baklava?"

"Good choice." Ahmet handed him a plate and shepherded him to a chair. Sitting, John reached for a small fork and gently pried off a miniscule bite, smiling awkwardly as the others stared. John's smile widened at the sweet-savory flavor of honey and nuts. "It's tasty," he said, wiping his mouth with a napkin.

"Good!" Ahmet leaned forward. "Where did you learn to read?"

John glanced around the room. He recognized multiple people from the previous night: Erik Rus, Beyzra, al-Haytham, and Andrew of the Soissens Conglomerate. He noticed that they had fallen silent, their gazes fixed on him. He closed his eyes with a sigh. "My father taught me."

"Your father? Was he also a hunter?"

"No, he was a merchant."

"What was his name?"

"I would rather not say."

"But he did have a family name, right?"

John clenched his jaw. "He did."

"As would you, I suppose. You said you didn't?"

John stayed silent.

"In House Husniye, we value honesty," Ahmet said.

"Then why didn't you tell me about how the heir for this gatestone works? Or how anything works?"

"Well, I apologize. I haven't had a free moment since Husniye's passing. Besides, the Spire heir system is common knowledge."

"For those who live on Spire Island. You also never mentioned that the gatekeeper of this stone is the head of the house." John held up Olumtahss and gazed about. He noticed Erik suppressing laughter behind a hand as everyone else stared, open-mouthed.

Ahmet turned to glare at Erik. Then he looked back at John, clearing his throat. "Declaring an heir can take a degree of training to do so correctly."

"I can handle it."

Erik Rus piped up. "Most of the spells that tie into the Spires system have rules. One is that you have to cast the spells willingly. We can't coerce you into anything. That's for declaring an heir, or even relinquishing it to the heir, if you want." He cheekily grinned as Ahmet gave him another stormy look.

"I can relinquish the stone?" John blurted.

"Of course you can," Erik replied. "Did you think we were going to kill you once you set an heir?"

John froze, eyes flitting from person to person. The silence spoke volumes.

He jumped at a booming laugh from Erik. Al-Haytham stepped forward. He gave John an encouraging smile. "I'll make sure to sit down and teach you anything you need to know. Meet me at the library tomorrow." He moved away to take a plate of baklava for himself.

Al-Haytham's movement broke the tension, and everyone else moved toward the tables. Soon the room filled with casual talk and laughter, and John took the opportunity to take another few bites of food. Then a young woman plopped down beside him and smiled through white teeth. "Hello there!"

John stared, bewildered.

"We met last night. I'm Roshan." She leaned forward, and he couldn't help but notice the ample cleavage that pressed against the fabric of her shirt.

He made himself glance away, mumbling, "Hello." Then he remembered. "You're Beyzra's daughter. The opal merchant."

"Oh, you do remember!" She beamed. "How do you find House Husniye?"

John shrugged, glancing around the room to avoid her gaze. As he did, he noticed that several of her family had already congregated nearby, blocking Ahmet from view.

Roshan twirled her hair around a finger, "Do you want to go for a walk? I bet no one has bothered to offer you a tour of the compound."

"Okay."

Grabbing his arm, she guided him from the room. In the hall, she pointed at the view through a nearby window.

"They built the whole building around a central garden here. The first floor is meeting rooms and dining halls. Think of it as a big rectangle, so if you get lost all you have to do is keep walking and you'll get there eventually".

"As long as you are on the right floor," John grunted.

Roshan giggled, pointing as they passed a large room, "The main dining area for the servants and soldiers. You don't need to worry about that one." Pulling him toward a turn, she went on. "There are stairs at the back two corners, so it's easy to go up and down. If you take a right here you will pass the kitchens, but we are going up instead."

At the top of the stairs, Roshan picked up her pace. "Over here is my favorite place."

They entered a cozy room filled with comfy looking armchairs. A man, reading in one of the chairs, ignored them as they entered. A motion caused John to start—a floating mage lamp. The room was full of them, each with its own rope. Roshan reached out to tug the rope attached to the closest lamp. It moved through the air. "It's so you can bring them closer if you are reading a book or something. Handy!"

"Is it safe?" John asked.

Roshan's head tilted. "Why wouldn't it be safe? Come on, let me show you the balcony!"

He let her tug him toward the back wall, which had an ornate stained-glass door. She opened the door and pulled him through. "Isn't it pretty?"

Below them, John glanced at greenery and flowers, giving a brief nod. To his right, Roshan leaned against the railing. "I always love coming here." She breathed. John grunted, and she looked over. "Not impressed?"

"No," he replied. "Sorry, I don't want to be rude. I just don't really want to be involved in all this."

"Why?"

"It's more stress than it's worth."

"I'm sorry. We can go back."

"I mean the whole situation is stressful. It's not anyone's fault." John scratched his beard. "Other than maybe Husniye's."

Roshan looked at him for a moment, then gave him an impish grin. One hand slid along the railing, and she laid a finger on his chest. She spoke softly, "Who do you want to make heir, then?"

John leaned backward.

They jumped as the stained-glass door swung open. Ahmet, flanked by two soldiers, stepped through. One was Cecil. "There you are! We were looking for you!"

Roshan bowed. "I was just giving him a tour of the house. Next stop is the basement."

Ahmet clapped his hands together. "Wonderful! We'll join you."

They all walked downstairs. "We do most of our magic here," Ahmet opened a door with a flourish. The room inside was dimly lit, massive, with stone columns interspersed throughout. Cabinets with hundreds of small drawers covered one wall. He saw moveable privacy screens and multiple platforms, some empty and others burdened by huge crystals. It didn't smell damp for a basement, John noticed.

Al-Haytham, seated at a desk, stood to greet them, smiling. "It took a lot of effort to set up too."

As John's eyes adjusted, he noticed figures moving in the shadows. The room was busy, yet there was very little noise. "Why the basement?" he asked.

"Better shielding," Al-Haytham motioned them through the door. "And it's farther away from everyone sleeping, so if there is a leak at night, nobody would be affected."

"Not that there is any danger, of course," Ahmet hurriedly added. "Just some extra precautions."

"Why is it so dark?"

Al-Haytham nodded. "Good question. It's easier to scry when it's dark, and it's easier to see what the magic is doing. Noticing slight changes in a glow helps tremendously when diagnosing issues with spellwork."

"What are you doing now?"

"Searching for Ece."

Another voice emerged from the shadows. "I have been thinking about our situation." John recognized it as Beyzra's. As she stepped into the dim mage light, John noticed her exchange a significant look with Roshan, who stood at his side. "To satisfy the Spire, John should consider declaring a temporary heir until we find her."

Al-Haytham responded, "He will need time to practice the spellwork."

"Why don't we let my daughter show him?" Beyzra gestured to Roshan.

Ahmet stepped between John and Roshan. "Of course, I would be willing to be designated temporary heir until we found Ece."

Beyza's voice rose, "I think it is clear that many here would be uncomfortable with that."

John stepped back. He sensed the conversation building to an argument in which he had no interest or energy given the hours-long tour. He shifted close to Cecil and whispered, "So this is where I would declare someone the heir, right?"

Cecil nodded. He nudged John playfully. "You were getting friendly with Roshan earlier, huh? She can be fun."

His grin faded as Beyzra's voice cut through. "Someone outside the leadership pool would be ideal. Roshan can manage …"

At this point, al-Haytham stepped forward. "Excuse me, this room is not for meetings. If you wish to discuss anything, do it upstairs."

"Shall we go back to the tea room?" Ahmet suggested.

"Of course," Beyrza agreed.

The two swept from the room, leaving John behind. With relief, he realized they had forgotten he was standing there. Roshan tugged at his sleeve, "I'll talk to you later!" She blew him a little kiss and hurried to follow.

As they left the magic room, the two heard raised voices echoing from the stairwell. "I'm sorry about that," Cecil said.

John let out a sigh of relief. "I am exhausted."

Cecil patted him gently on the shoulder. "Why don't we get you some dinner and an early bed."

"That sounds great. What did they mean by satisfy the Spire?"

"Gatekeepers have to declare an heir within thirty days, or else the Spire can confiscate the stone," Cecil said, shrugging. "It's been a source of constant drama."

"Thirty days? How many days has it been?" John tried to count, but everything had been a blur.

Al-Haytham interjected, "Get some sleep. We can talk about it tomorrow morning."

"Can I eat dinner in my room?" John asked as they took the stairs up.

"Sure, I'll have someone drop by some food for you."

"Thanks."

# 6

Cecil awoke in his private room, a benefit of being a captain. He rolled out of bed for a few quick stretches and glanced out the window. The sky had just started to brighten. Moving quickly, he shaved, used the restroom, activated the magic seal above the toilet to whisk his waste away, and dressed in casual, simple clothing.

He entered the barracks. As expected, most of the beds were empty, many of the men being assigned to various holdings around House Husniye. The twelve garrisoned in the main house were already awake and dressed. Grateful he didn't have to yell at anybody today, he barked, "Meet in the courtyard in five," and headed down himself.

The weather on Spire Island was temperate, differences between winter and summer almost negligible. In the morning, before the sun warmed everything, the air was cool, perfect for a workout. He led the men through some stretches, a jog around the courtyard, and basic combat drills, then dismissed them. Back in his room, he bathed and assumed his dress uniform. Upon returning to John's room, he heard Ahu inside, helping John get ready for the day. He knocked on the door, making sure his uniform was on straight.

John opened the door quickly, dressed and clean for the day, looking sullen as always. Cecil glanced at Ahu, who gave him a thumbs-up. "Good morning, I hope you slept well."

"Someone locked me in my room last night," John replied.

Cecil made a face. "Yes, I suppose they didn't want you wandering around without an escort."

"What, don't they trust me? Even after that lovely dinner?"

Cecil eyed him, trying to decide if the hunter was joking or not. "They don't really know you." Seeing John's expression, Cecil cracked a smile. "Right, let's get some food, and head over to al-Haytham." As they left, Ahu was already busy re-making John's bed.

In the library, books of every shape and language overflowed the shelves and onto piles on tables. Cecil stood at attention near the door, watching John peruse the various titles.

"He should be here soon," Cecil stated. "He isn't much of a morning person."

John nodded, grabbed a book at random from the table next to him, and read, *A Study of Tree Bellers*. An image of a teal bird with four eyes graced the cover. Cecil sidled over to look over John's shoulder. After a moment, John looked up at him.

"That's a pretty advanced book." Cecil studied the dense language.

John shrugged. "I used to read Anderson's medical books. He's a friend of mine."

"Why?"

"Ran out of other books to read." John demurred, going back to his book. Cecil gave him a quick side-eye, then returned to his position by the door. A few moments later, a half-asleep al-Haytham shuffled into the room.

"Good morning. Sorry I am late."

"Not a problem," John said, placing the book open on the table.

"Well, I suppose it's my job to teach you about the gatestones then. What do you know?"

"Not much."

Al-Haytham nodded and wordlessly headed to a shelf to pull down a text.

"What did it mean by 'induced'?" John asked, pointing at the book he had just put down.

"Ah, infused with magic. Sort of like a Twisted, but on purpose." Al-Haytham absentmindedly flipped through his own book. Finding the page he was looking for, he sat on the chair opposite John. Dust wafted up and hung in a sunbeam. "So assuming you know nothing …" He appeared to notice what John had been reading for the first time, and Cecil saw him glance quickly up at the hunter. "I'll start with the basics. Magic or Storm, as you know it, is controlled through will. The gatestones are made with magic and are used in a massive network of communication and transportation. Using the gatestone to send a message or an object requires an exertion of will from somebody. Good so far?"

John nodded.

"Good. If there's no will behind something infused with magic, eventually it will disintegrate. Understand?"

John pointed to his open book. "How do the tree bellers not disintegrate then?"

Al-Haytham grinned. "Ah ha! Yes, the birds exert a will on themselves. Thus, they avoid destruction. But, uh, don't mention that to anyone. That fact should not be known widely. It could have repercussions. Yes?"

As John nodded, Cecil attempted to catch al-Haytham's eye and send a silent warning.

"Anyway, where was I? Let us talk about gatestones. The houses have contracts with the Spire to provide gatestones. Like all magic creations, these require constant will. They are also difficult to create. Thus, there are rules to keep them from crumbling. Any keeper of the stone, henceforth referred to as a gatekeeper, is to have an heir. If the gatekeeper was to die or become exhausted to the point they could no longer perform their duties, the responsibility of maintaining the stone is immediately passed to the heir. The heir then must hold the gatestone together and name an heir as well. Of course, most stones require multiple keepers because maintaining their power requires more will than a single person can provide. All this is enforced by the Spire, to ensure that the gatestones don't crumble. What do you know about the Spire?"

"Assume I know nothing," John said.

Al-Haytham chuckled. "Using my own words against me. Quite skillful wordplay from a hermit. I'm surprised you even remember how to speak!"

John took his comment as teasing, not malice, and Cecil took note of his smile. "It's not like I never talk to anyone. I often visit Anderson, a doctor in the nearest town. Educated at the university in the capital."

"Well, he certainly knows how to choose his company. Now, as for the Spire. They originally created the … hmm …" Al-Haytham considered how much to reveal to this stranger. "No, I think I will tell you the accurate history. The Spire started as a loose organization of mages that had created gatestones for their own purposes. They wanted to be able to use each other's gatestones, so they made deals, eventually forming an extensive network. Kingdoms, warlords, and merchants all wanted the power to travel where they pleased. So the mages began selling their services as a teleportation network. Eventually, they organized the Spire as we know it. Anyone with their own gatestone network was absorbed into the Spire, willingly or otherwise. Do you understand?"

John furrowed his eyebrows. "I thought the gatestones were run by the local nobility?"

"It's complicated, but often the local nobles subcontract out the creation and running of gatestones. It gets political, but the houses in the Spire provide a service, running stones on behalf of other groups. Our house is only contracted for about a dozen, depending on how you count them, not including the stone we own outright in the basement, or that." Al-Haytham pointed at the stone around John's neck. "Your stone is special. It requires only one gatekeeper, and it is the smallest gatestone known. The second smallest is the size of a child, I believe."

John held the stone up to the light. "Li mentioned something like that."

"Li? Ah, from House Wu. I suspect there are others like it, but the Spire controls them. They hold many secrets in their tower. I would love to visit their library someday," al-

Haytham replied. "Anyhow, those are the basics. Any questions?"

"How is it so small? Is it because it's a soulstone?" John asked.

"Ah, no. It has a strong connection to the aether. The ancient lich who created it made it a powerful source of magic. Unlike most spellstones, which are passive, the soulstone actively pumps magic in from the aether, so it produces far more magic than it should, given its size."

"Lich?" John asked.

"Oh. Someone who has figured out how to cheat death. Without replacing their body, that is," al-Haytham added. "It's complicated, but you can think of it almost like placing your soul into the gem instead of having it in your body. Well, more a copy of your soul? A simulacrum of your mind, you see."

"So, is his soul still inside here?"

"Oh, no. Husniye ripped that out. As far as I understand it, she simply used it as the raw material to create Olumtahss, much like reforging a sword into a plow."

"Oh. Good." John tucked the stone back into his tunic. "Right, one more question. How do I set an heir?"

"Right to the point! It's simple. You will it." Al-Haytham gave a dry laugh at John's expression. "It requires concentration and knowledge of the contract you are setting in place. A tool called a circle helps with such things. The fact you can read makes this far easier. Here." Al-Haytham handed John the book he had unshelved earlier.

At that moment, another Husniye soldier entered and whispered to Cecil, "Ahmet wants to speak to you."

"Stay here," he ordered the man. Leaving John in al-Haytham's care, Cecil headed out.

Cecil took his time getting to Ahmet—first visiting the restroom, then getting a cup of water. Outside Ahmet's door, he hesitated again, re-checking his uniform before knocking. Ahmet put his pen down and with a broad sweep of his hand directed Cecil to the one open chair. "Cecil! Good to see you. Have a seat! How are things going with John?"

"He's doing fine. He's smart for a hermit who lives in the woods."

"Yes, interesting, isn't it? I wanted to speak to you about Alriyh."

Cecil grimaced. "What happened now?"

"No need to worry, but there has been a change in policy. He's no longer allowed in the house."

Cecil's jaw dropped. "His family has been part of this house for as long as Husniye has!"

"Cecil, listen. The situation here has evolved quickly."

"That's not the point ..." Cecil began.

Ahmet slammed the table. "I don't need this right now, Cecil. Please."

Cecil made no reply but held Ahmet's eye.

The other man broke first. "Do we have an understanding?"

"Yes, sir." Cecil stood to leave.

"One more thing," Ahmet said. Cecil sat down. "Keep an eye on John for me. I want him to stay in the building, and let me know if anyone talks to him."

"Of course," Cecil said, a little too quickly.

Ahmet slid a pair of spellstones across the table, two flat disks carved with intricate spellwork. "Here are two short-range communication stones. They're linked."

Ahmet gave him a knowing look. Without acknowledging Ahmet's intent, Cecil grabbed the stones, slid them into his pocket, and stood in one movement. "Yes, sir, of course." He left the office, closing the door behind him.

Before returning to John, Cecil sought out Ahu. He waved her down as she organized the laundry for the day. "Ahu," he called from the door, interrupting her conversation with another woman.

"Yes?" Ahu answered, annoyed.

"Alriyh just got kicked out of the house." His heart lurched as he said it.

"I know."

"You do?"

"Did you really not see this coming?" she asked, softly.

Cecil sighed, making eye contact with the wall.

Ahu continued. "Are you okay?"

"No, I grew up with him. I remember playing tag with him on my birthday."

"It's politics, Cecil."

"Fuck politics," Cecil said, a little too loudly. Ahu gently touched his shoulder. He took a deep breath. "Right, sorry. I should get back to work."

"Keep your head down," Ahu said. "We'll get through this."

"This wouldn't have happened if Husniye was alive."

"This happened because Husniye is no longer alive," Ahu corrected, then patted him on the shoulder. "Just keep trying your best."

Cecil nodded and headed off.

Cecil tapped the guard on the shoulder, giving him a small nod to leave, leaving Cecil to stand at attention and watch John read the book, approaching closer and craning his neck to see the text until al-Haytham approached. Cecil resumed his position at the door.

Al-Haytham sat across from John with a thump. "So, quiz time. What's the grace period before a gatestone is seized by the Spire, if an heir is not set?" John glanced up. "Without looking."

"One month?"

Al-Haytham clapped his hands. "Wonderful! Which means that within a month, you need to set an heir, or else the Spire will strip you of your stone. Which would make many people unhappy."

"Why didn't they tell me about making an heir right away then?"

"Because once you know how to set an heir, you might choose someone outside of House Husniye. They wanted to make sure they had your loyalty first."

Cecil gave al-Haytham another warning look but got only a wry smile in return.

John rolled his eyes. "I figured it was something like that. I just want out of here."

"Oh, it's obvious what you want. Ahmet is used to dealing with greed, though, not someone so austere. Now then, another question. I believe this one pertains to you.

How can a gatekeeper be stripped of their stone and contract?"

John allowed himself a small smile. Al-Haytham reminded him of Anderson with his love of knowledge and books.

"The … something entity has to petition the Spire?" John hesitated.

"Subcontracting entity. That one was a bit of a trick question. The Spire holds the right to strip any gatekeeper of a gatestone at any time."

"Wait, what?"

"Ah, just because they can doesn't mean they will. They technically can, but if they do so without the permission of the house or a good reason, there would be a major uproar."

Cecil watched John take this in.

"Who defines a good reason?"

"Basically anything that doesn't anger the houses!" Al-Haytham waved his hands theatrically.

"So if someone is unpopular, the Spire can do whatever they want to them?"

"Ahh, but rampant abuse by the Spire may also upset some."

"It sounds political."

"It is quite political, yes. As described, the house petitions the Spire, and the Spire strips a specific gatekeeper from that house of their stone. The only time the Spire is supposed to strip a gatekeeper without a house's petition is if the gatekeeper is blocking traffic from, let's say, a rival subcontractor running a different stone."

"So the houses are the subcontractors?"

"Ah, yes. They assist the Spire in running the gate transportation network. The Spire makes most gatestones. Yours is an exception. Husniye acquired the raw stone, then modified it heavily."

"So this stone isn't part of the Spire network?"

"It is, but it isn't. The Spire did not create it, so the magic contracts on it differ. It still can access the Spire's transportation network, but it can also do things outside the Spire's control, a point of sore contention."

"Why didn't they strip it from Husniye then?"

"She was good at politics," al-Haytham said, a slight smile dancing on his lips. Al-Haytham grabbed a book titled *Basics of Spellcircles*.

"Unfortunately, I have a meeting I need to go to, but this should cover everything you need to create a spellcircle for declaring an heir."

"Right." As John grabbed the book, Cecil watched al-Haytham bow to the hunter, then leave.

Pausing after reading the same page three times, John turned to Cecil. "Are you okay?"

"I'm not supposed to leave you alone."

"Do you need to go to the bathroom?"

"I'm fine." Cecil stayed at attention.

"That didn't answer my question."

"I'm fine," Cecil repeated.

John went back to reading, but half a page later, he paused again. "Aren't you the captain or something?"

"Yes, but Ahmet wanted me to handle this personally," Cecil insisted.

The door to the library burst open, startling them both. Andrew of Soissens strode in. "Hello, John, I was hoping to speak with you."

Cecil was already in motion, stepping between them.

Andrew glared at Cecil. "Excuse me."

"I'm sorry, he's busy studying magic."

"I just need a moment."

"It's very important that he is allowed to study uninterrupted."

Andrew put a hand on Cecil's shoulder. "Were you aware that Ahmet has made me a director of House Husniye?"

Cecil hesitated. "I was aware of that, yes."

Cecil let Andrew gently push past. "John, would you mind coming with me for a moment?" Andrew gestured to the hallway.

John clenched his jaw and nodded. He rose to follow the other man, and as he walked past, Cecil slipped a communication stone into the wide pocket of his loose tunic. John gave no sign of noticing.

The second they were out of sight, Cecil scrambled for the other stone. He held it to his ear.

"So, what did you want to talk to me about?" John's voice was loud, as if he was holding the stone up to his face.

He barely heard Andrew's reply. "Let's step in here." The door to the next room in the passage opened and closed. Andrew's voice was clear. "Would you like anything to drink?"

"No thanks." John's voice was quieter now. There was the rustling of clothes. John must be sitting. Cecil closed his eyes, concentrating.

"You have had quite the week, haven't you?"

"I'm fine."

"Well, just let me know if you need anything. Other than the massive upheaval in your life, how have you been doing?"

"Fine, I suppose."

"Good, good. Are you planning to head back to your home after this is resolved?"

"Yes."

"Maybe I can help with that. You have acquired quite the valuable artifact. I doubt you will be able to return to your normal life while you are still bound to Olumtahss. The only way you can get rid of it is by giving it away or selling it."

Cecil winced at the word sell.

Andrew continued. "House Husniye wants the gatestone to pass to Ece, who is currently missing. Who knows how long it will take for them to find her, and that leaves you in a strange position. I can set up the spellcircles and assistants that will let you declare a new heir, outside of House Husniye. In exchange, I will make sure you are well looked after."

"You want me to sell you Olumtahss."

"You get to go home with a sackful of coins, or a land deed, or whatever you want really. Let me know your price."

Behind Cecil, Al-Haytham walked in. "Where's John?"

Cecil flapped his hand at him in a panic, then pointed a finger at the stone pressed to his ear. Andrew continued to speak. "—worried about reprisal, don't be. Once you are no longer the gatekeeper, you aren't of much interest to anybody. No offense. You get to walk away from all of this."

Cecil heard John. "What about House Husniye?"

"They will continue to exist, of course. Why?"

"I don't want to screw over a bunch of people for money," John muttered.

"Any choice you make will screw someone over. It's just a question of who."

Al-Haytham stood next to Cecil, questions on his face. Cecil ignored him as Andrew sighed. "I'll tell you what. If at any time you want to talk about it, come to the Soissens office. Ahmet pointed it out on your tour, right? Fantastic. Think about it and let me know."

Outside, the door opened again, and Cecil slipped the receiving stone back into his pocket. Seconds later, John walked in. Returning to the table, he tossed something at Cecil. "Here's your spy stone back." He sat at the table and pulled his book toward him. "You are really terrible at subterfuge."

Cecil felt himself blushing. "I know." His shoulders slumped.

Behind them, al-Haytham gave a hearty laugh.

⌒

John flopped into bed, covering his eyes.

"Do you want me to arrange dinner?" Cecil asked.

John nodded and added, "I'm impressed you could focus for so long."

"I want to get out of here. No offense."

"None taken."

John suddenly sat upright. "I want to make a trip. I want to visit Riverside."

"Riverside?"

"I ... grew up there. There is someone I need to talk to."

"Riverside, the big city, run by House Romanov?"

John nodded.

"May I ask why?"

"My old priest. I ... just need to talk to someone."

Cecil pursed his lips. "I can guarantee that Ahmet wouldn't allow it, especially since a different house operates the gate network."

John appeared to collapse in on himself. Cecil saw tears welling in the man's eyes. John wiped at his face. "Sorry, sorry. It's just been a ... day. Week. I don't even know."

Cecil shifted from foot to foot. "The Storm Church?"

"Church of the Clear Sky, yeah."

Cecil nodded. "I don't think you will be allowed to go to Riverside."

"Wait!" John whipped out Olumtahss. "Can't I use this to travel there?"

"Well, if you know how, you can, but the stone would be left behind. You can't use a stone to send itself, if that makes sense."

"Can you just look after it while I go there?"

"You would be leaving the protection the stone gives you, and I don't know how you would get back. And, of course, everyone would throw a fit if you did that, but there is a church on Spire Island, if you want to talk to the priest there."

"I would really like that."

"I'll talk to Ahmet. See if I can arrange something." He hesitated, hand on the door. "They'll probably lock the door again tonight. And I'm sure Ahmet wants someone posted outside. Sorry." Cecil closed the door behind him.

# 7

John and Cecil's morning walk was uneventful. Ahmet had been resistant at first, but Cecil reminded him that the Spire had several protections for gatekeepers. Al-Haytham also pointed out that Olumtahss provided its own protections. So Ahmet relented, even letting him go with just Cecil.

The church itself was an impressive building. Painted stone carvings adorned the front. Above the doorway, a beautiful mural depicted a rising sun driving away storm clouds. John felt better just looking at it. Two stout men in uniform flanked the door. John acknowledged them with a quizzical glance at Cecil. "They are wearing Spire colors."

"They have to follow the same rules as everyone else on this island."

"Oh." John hesitated before heading in.

Inside, a female, who appeared to be about twelve, greeted them in a white dress with a wreath of flowers on her head. "Welcome to the Storm Church!" She gave a small curtsy.

Cecil broke into a grin, putting his hands on his knees and leaning forward to respond. "Why, hello there! Mr. John Hunter here would like to talk to one of your priests."

"Okay, mister!" She raced off.

A moment later, an older man in a white robe ducked through a doorway and walked toward them. He held out his open palms. "May the Storm always be on the horizon."

"And never above your head," John finished, also clapping his hands together and giving a small bow. The man flung his arms out and gave them both a smile.

"My name is Father Gregory. What can I do for you today?"

"Hello, Father Gregory, I could use some advice."

"Of course! Follow me, if you please." He gestured to another door and stepped forward to open it. John moved to walk through. The priest held up a palm when Cecil tried to follow. "I am afraid you are going to have to stay here. No weapons allowed in the church proper, and correct me if I am wrong, but you are not a believer. Please wait here."

Cecil caught the door to stop it from closing. "I need to stay with John the entire time."

Father Gregory winked. "I can promise nothing will happen to him. What harm can come from a cup of tea?"" He pushed Cecil's hand from the door and closed it.

Cecil stared at the closed door for a moment, then sighed. "I guess I'll wait here then."

John let the steam from a mug of tea bathe his face. Father Gregory sat across from him and waited for him to speak. Eventually, John eventually pulled the gatestone out from under his shirt, letting it dangle.

Father Gregory nodded. "I have heard about what happened. I'm sorry you have to deal with this."

"I don't know what to do."

"Normally I would never give this kind of advice, but this is … an unusual situation. Think of yourself first. You were pulled into this without any say on the matter, and there are many out there who would want to use you as a tool."

"But …" John clenched his fist. "They aren't what I expected. A lot of them are nice. And they care."

"What do you mean?"

John locked eyes with the priest. "This is Spire Island. A place of great evil, where Storm flows freely, ancient mages practice unholy magic. It is the source of many of the Twisted that rampage across the lands. But many of the people here don't seem evil."

Gregory leaned back. "Many don't view this as a place of evil. They believe the Spire is our savior, forcing all the mages to follow safety regulations." He held up a hand as John opened his mouth to speak. "That's a common view here, that the Spire is on the side of good, helping control the use of Storm and to curb the damage it can do. That they are good people, trying to help the world heal from wounds brought on by Storm."

John stared into his mug. "That's a false choice. If you choose the lesser of two evils, you are still choosing an evil. Why not stop the use of Storm, cleanse the land of Twisted, and retake this world for humanity?"

"Storm is much like fire," Gregory began, but John scoffed and cut him off.

"I've heard this before. Useful. Only dangerous if let loose. The difference is that fire can destroy a house or a town. But Storm can turn you into a monster and leave an area uninhabitable for centuries."

"Hah, true. Let me put it another way. We, as a people, have become dependent on Storm. We need fertility stones, we need the healers, and we need the transportation. Choices made before our time made us reliant on it. Our choice is how to proceed. If all Storm vanished overnight, many would die. Wouldn't trying to contain the damage be far better than causing such a catastrophe?"

"Yes, but the Spire takes things too far. They use Storm not just to survive, but for luxury."

"It's difficult to draw the line between luxury and survival. If someone is injured, but can still work, would it be a sin to heal them? I do not think so." The priest raised an eyebrow at John. "Some argue otherwise."

"I don't think controlling people's minds and using them as slaves is anything but a luxury and a sin."

Gregory winced and rubbed his chin. "Yes, there is that. The Spire cares more about Storm being used safely, not how it's used. It's their biggest fault."

"I don't see that changing. The Spire has no morals. They operate on greed and politics. Whether or not to use Storm should be a moral question, not a mercantile one."

Gregory considered John. "You are more educated than I would have thought."

"My dad made sure I had a solid education, and I like to read."

"So should the church oversee mages instead of the Spire?"

John rested his head on his fist, thinking before he gave a slow reply: "I don't think the grand temple will do much better. They charge a fee for indulging in Storm and often turn a blind eye to what you do with it if you pay enough."

John saw the priest's hand tighten on the arm of his chair. "Have you ever heard of Sunray?"

John snorted. "Those lunatics? I don't think running around killing mages and blowing up gatestones will help anybody."

Gregory relaxed. "The point I was trying to make is many involved in the Spire are good people just trying to make the best of a difficult situation. Having said that, I don't believe you are obligated to help them."

"Why?"

"This is Spire business. The Spire designed the heir system for gatestones specifically to avoid gatestones without gatekeepers; therefore, the Spire oversees it. Correct me if I am wrong, but you never asked to work for the Spire. This isn't something an outsider should deal with."

John was silent.

"I may know someone who can help you." Father Gregory stood. "Please, follow me. I'll make the introduction."

Cecil tapped his foot, staring at the artwork on the wall. With no clock in the room, Cecil was forced to estimate time. The sun had almost reached its zenith, and his growing hunger pangs told him it must be noon.

The priest stepped into the room, acknowledging him with a nod. Cecil shot to his feet, noting John's absence.

"John went to have lunch with a friend. He'll meet you back at House Husniye."

"Oh, absolutely not. No offense, sir, but I've been ordered to be with him at all times. I am going to need to know where this lunch is taking place."

"Perhaps, sir, you should give him space. He has been through a lot recently, and—" He was cut off.

"With all due respect," Cecil's voice rose, "I am more worried about the priceless artifact he has around his neck, which I am sure he told you about. Sure, John is in a shit situation, but I have my duties. I need to know where he is right now."

The priest bowed and turned to a large man who had just walked in through a side entrance, "Shay, please escort this gentleman out of the building."

"Of course, sir."

Cecil sized the man up. He was tall, muscled. His dark skin contrasted with his white robe. He carried a curved saber and a buckler on his belt. Cecil's eyes narrowed. The light didn't bounce off the metal like it would off steel. Both the buckler and saber were null-infused. A church on Spire Island would have access to such material.

Cecil pulled his longsword out of his scabbard. His weapon, inscribed with magic that enhanced its cutting ability, would be of limited use against a null-infused buckler. In addition, Shay also drew a null-infused saber and assumed a combat pose.

Father Gregory cleared his throat. "We don't have to resort to violence. Shay here is quite skilled. I think it's best for everyone here if you just put your sword back in its scabbard and leave."

Cecil also took a combat stance. "I just want to know where the lunch is taking place."

"Very well." The priest nodded and Shay launched himself forward.

Cecil took advantage of the longer reach of his sword, keeping it in front of him. Shay moved quickly, pushing Cecil's blade to the side with his buckler, trying to get his own saber in range. Cecil took a small step back, brought his sword around the small shield, realigned the point with Shay's thick neck, then thrust it forward. Shay retreated and took a new stance with the saber high and the buckler forward. They both paused a moment, catching their breath.

"Not going to be that easy," Cecil taunted. Shay said nothing. Cecil waited, sword at his hip, pointing toward Shay almost casually.

He wasn't waiting long. Shay crouched, knees angled, legs spread wide. With his long legs, he lunged forward. As he closed the distance, Cecil thrust the point toward Shay's chest, trying to rotate the longsword to catch the incoming saber. But Shay had closed the distance more than Cecil thought. At the last moment, Cecil yanked his arms away and jumped back, his sword clanging against the buckler. They both paused again, panting.

Cecil glanced at his arm and saw blood. If he hadn't pulled back in time, he could have lost a hand at the wrist. He narrowed his eyes and changed his stance. The roof was high enough not to worry about catching his sword, so he raised his weapon as if to bring it down on his opponent's head. Shay raised his saber in response.

This time, Cecil lunged forward. Shay met him, moving to catch the incoming blade, and twisting his saber around toward Cecil's belly. As his blade tapped the buckler, Cecil changed direction, arcing it to one side with the tip pointing down and his hands still high. His leg muscles flexing with the effort, Cecil arrested his forward momentum. With a backward step, he narrowly avoided being disemboweled, while aiming for Shay's leg.

They parted again, and Cecil saw Shay glance down at a growing patch of red on his calf. He looked at the priest, who growled, "You're an animal, you know that?"

Cecil smiled at him. "Heard many a woman say that."

Gregory made a choking noise, looked at his wounded guardsman, and sighed. "They are at the Flirty Cod. Get out of my temple."

"Thank you." Cecil took a few steps back before sheathing his sword. Shay did the same, not breaking eye contact.

Cecil paused at the door and turned to wave at Shay. "If you ever want to spar, come on by House Husniye. You're good." He flashed a smile and left.

⌒

John trailed a server into a small back room of the restaurant and stopped short. "Oh."

Trey sat at a small round table in a round room. Throughout the room, guards stood at attention before walls painted with beautiful murals of fishing scenes in natural landscapes. The man who had been escorting John pulled a chair back and motioned for him to sit. John glanced at the stern faces of the guards, swords at their sides, and sat, tentatively.

"I didn't really expect this."

Trey's smile failed to reach his eyes. "This is a favorite restaurant of mine. I figured we could have a friendly conversation over lunch."

John studied Trey's expensive clothes: high boots, a deep-blue shirt, and a black vest embroidered with the two towers of his house. He cast his gaze to the table. "She really did ask me to tell you that. Those were her dying words."

"Is that so?" Trey sipped wine as a server placed a glass in front of John. He poured as John gestured for him to stop.

"So you just did as she asked, then?"

"I suppose so."

"You suppose so." Trey set the wineglass down with a soft clink. "Hell of a thing to say to someone who you just met for the first time, isn't it?" he breathed.

John clenched his jaw and said nothing.

"Well, let us discuss your ... current goals in life. What are you trying to achieve by involving yourself in this?"

"I didn't ask to get involved in this."

Trey smiled and in a light tone said, "I would gladly take it off of you if you wanted."

"I don't know if that is a good idea."

"Why's that?"

"Husniye told me to hold on to the stone. And not to trust anyone. I'm involved now."

"Yes, she wants you to act as a courier for her problems. Which is unfortunate, because you seem to be out of your league." John continued to stare at the table. "Are you from outside the walls?"

"I'm not a wild man."

"That isn't what I asked." Trey leaned forward.

"The natural nullstone fields near Riverside. No walls needed. The stone keeps things at bay."

"You live in that accursed place?" Trey replied with a laugh. "It can take almost twenty acres to feed one family! Listen, you obviously don't have much experience with magic. We can sort this out. Let me take the gem, and you can start heading home. I think you'll find I am a generous man." He held up a money pouch and shook it. Coins clinked inside.

John let him wait for a few moments before asking, "So what am I involved with then?"

"Nothing that should concern you."

"Well, I'm concerning myself."

Trey sighed. "Husniye gave you something she shouldn't have, is all."

"You know what else Husniye did?" John met Trey's eyes at last. "Husniye told me to tell you to go fuck yourself."

Some guards shifted uncomfortably, while Trey forced a smile and then signaled the waitstaff. "Why don't we order some food?"

Cecil leaned against a wall and glanced around the corner to look at a specific building. Above the door hung a sign depicting codfish on a plate surrounded by lettuce leaves.

With its long eyelashes, puckered red lips, and coquettish wink, The Flirty Cod was an apt name.

Three men in chain mail shirts and helmets and brandishing longswords stood under the sign. They wore dyed tunics, solid blue with two white towers on their chests. House DuFort colors. The guardsmen of one Jacques Maxamillion the Third. Trey to his enemies. Of course Trey was behind this.

"It had to be him. Ahmet is going to kill me." Cecil shook his head. He took stock of his red clothing—obvious Husniye colors. He sidled away from the corner, then sauntered down the alleyway. One rune on the wall glowed, and Cecil slipped passed it, pressing himself against the opposite wall. Finally, he popped out into the back street.

The mood here was different, rougher. It smelled vaguely like shit. There were no mage lamps, no magic-canceling runes embedded in the walls. A few teamsters came by carrying bags or chests over their shoulders. Bottles rattled in the back of passing horse-drawn carriages.

While Cecil strolled along, some younger teamsters stopped to gawk at his sword. Most turned their gaze downward. Some of the older men urged the youngsters to stop staring and get back to work. Within a few strides, Cecil turned the corner to the rear of the restaurant and walked straight into another guard wearing a blue tunic.

The guard hesitated a moment, and Cecil punched him in the stomach. As the man doubled over, gasping, Cecil pulled a rod from his belt and pressed it into the back of the soldier's head. The rod glowed, and the man collapsed.

Cecil glanced behind him. Another knot of teamsters stared.

"Don't worry about it. He just had a visit from the sleepytime rod. Understand? Go about your day, please." Waving, Cecil stepped over the sleeping soldier and into the restaurant before anyone could yell for help.

Inside, he let his eyes adjust. The heat of the kitchen hit him in the face, and a boy carrying dishes stopped to ogle. Cecil held a finger to his lips and strode forward. As he made his way down the cramped hallway, his sword clattered against pots. A waiter stepped in front of him.

"Uh, sir, you can't be back here," the waiter stammered.

Cecil firmly nudged him aside. "I know." He stepped through the doorway, suddenly surrounded by light and chatter. He was in the main dining room, and around him groups ate at round tables. Another waiter, balancing four plates of steaming food on her arms, spotted him. She stared for a second, hurriedly served her plates to the table nearest her, then took off toward a side hallway. Cecil heard the man say, "I didn't order this?"

She reached the hallway first with Cecil close behind. He saw her waving at a guard at the end of the hallway and grabbed her arm. Murmuring a quick, "Sorry," he took three long strides, dragging her along.

The guard stood from his wooden chair and managed to yell, "Hey!"

Cecil threw the woman toward him. She took one stumbling step, then smacked straight into the guard's chest. He instinctively caught her, and they both fell backward tripping on a chair and sprawling across the ground.

Cecil stepped over them and reached for the door. Just as he was about to touch the handle, the door opened out, almost smacking him in the face. The guard on the other side of the door started, already pulling his sword out of his scabbard. In one motion, Cecil placed both hands on the man's wrist, forcing the sword back down, and headbutted him in the face. There was a crunch as the crown of Cecil's head slammed into the man's nose, and the guard went down hard.

Cecil stepped into a small room with an elegant chandelier and walls painted with fishing murals. In the center, at a table for two, sat John and Trey. Both looked surprised to see him. Trey held a forkful of fish halfway to his mouth.

"Hello, Trey. Nice to see you again." Cecil strode past the stunned guards, grabbed John by the arm, and hauled him out of his chair. "John, time to go."

The response was the whisper of steel on wood as guards drew swords from scabbards. As he turned to run, Cecil heard Trey yell, "Grab him!"

Cecil pulled John down the hallway, dragging him past the guard on the ground, who grabbed at their ankles. Cecil dissuaded him with a quick kick.

"Are you hurt?"

"No."

"Do you still have your gatestone?" He steered them through the dining area.

"Yes."

Cecil let go of John's arm. He glanced at the door to the kitchen, which was blocked by someone carrying a load of dishes. He veered out the front door with John at his heels.

"Hey!" One of the guards by the front door yelled as they burst out. Cecil drew his sword, took a step, and swung it at the man's head. The flat of the blade struck his helmet with a sound like a bell ringing, and the soldier sat down, blinking. They veered left, pedestrians scattering. Behind them, Trey's guardsmen shouted.

A few minutes later, they stopped at a street corner, bent over and wheezing, their pursuers having given up blocks ago.

Between gasping breaths, John said, "I'm sorry about that. I thought ..."

"It's fine." A few breaths later, Cecil added, "I should have kept a better eye on you."

John got his breathing under control. "He wanted the gatestone."

"Makes sense. Olumtahss is priceless."

"I remember."

"This way." Cecil pointed.

John followed him.

"So what would happen if I just ran off right now?"

"I suppose I would chase you down and drag you back."

"So not much different from Trey?"

Cecil gave John a sly grin. "I'm far more handsome and charming." He slapped John on the back. "Don't worry, we will get this sorted out quickly."

"Sure."

"Oh, and do me a favor. Don't tell anyone this happened."

John gave him a look. "Really?"

"Well, I didn't follow Ahmet's explicit instructions to never take my eyes off you, and I am sure if he found out there would be an explosion. Frankly, I don't want to deal with that right now."

John blinked a few times, then chuckled. "All right. Sure. But that's two favors you owe me."

Cecil paused, confused. "Two?" Then he grimaced. "Right. My drunken visit. I have not been making good decisions lately, let me tell you."

"Well, I didn't eat much. Can we go back and grab some food?"

Cecil nodded and turned to lead John back to House Husniye.

"Your arm's bleeding."

"Yeah, I know."

# 8

John leaned against the wall watching Ahu put the finishing touches on the bandage on Cecil's arm. They had made it back to Cecil's room with nobody asking too many questions. Ahu patted Cecil's arm. "How does that feel?"

Cecil smiled. "Fantastic, thank you."

Now Ahu scowled. "So how did you get that?"

Cecil glanced down. "I snagged it on some metal."

Ahu stared holes in Cecil. "You have that look on your face."

"What look?"

"The one you always have when you are lying."

"No I don't," Cecil replied, face flushing.

Ahu's eyes narrowed, and Cecil suddenly found the floor interesting. "Cecil?" said Ahu.

"There may have been some trouble." He scuffed the floor with his shoe.

"What happened?" Ahu eyed John next, who perused a bookshelf.

Cecil leaned forward, clasping his hands together. "Don't tell Ahmet."

"Oh no, that bad?" Ahu chewed her cheek.

"Promise not to tell," Cecil pleaded.

"If he doesn't need to know, I won't tell him."

"That's …" Cecil began, glanced up at Ahu's face, then groaned a little. "John may have been a little kidnapped."

Ahu's reply was louder than Cecil would have liked. "He may have been WHAT?"

"It's fine, it all worked out." Cecil gripped her hands, eyes pleading with her to keep it a secret.

"Is anybody dead?"

"No, nobody died."

Ahu let out a sigh of relief. "And you're okay, John?" They both looked toward the bookshelf, but John was no longer there. They shared a worried glance.

"Is he in the bathroom?" Cecil turned in his chair to examine the bathroom door.

"I don't think so…." Ahu crossed the room to knock on the door. "John?" She waited a moment before opening it. "Nope."

"Where did … wait." Cecil stood and crossed to the bookshelf. "The box is gone."

Ahu glowered at him. "What box?"

Cecil grimaced. "I had a box of some magic supplies on my bookshelf, and it's not there anymore."

Ahu headed to the door. "Let's find him before he does something stupid."

⌒

John wasn't hard to track down. Everyone in the hallways had taken note as the power walked past them without an escort. They followed his trail to the library first, where a tip from a serving girl led Cecil to check Ahmet's office. Inside, he spotted John furiously scribbling on the floor with chalk. Ahmet, behind his desk, watched, annoyed.

Cecil stepped inside. "Hey John, what's going on?" He exchanged a look with Ahmet, who frowned at John. Cecil gave a quick nod and stepped closer. "Hey, everything okay? What are you doing?"

John glanced between a book and his chalk drawings, muttering to himself. By now, a small crowd had gathered in the hallway, including al-Haytham, who stepped inside for a closer look. "That's imbued chalk."

Cecil turned, eyes wide. "Imbued chalk? Oh, that's a spellcircle." Everyone watching took a few steps back, and Ahmet leaned back in his chair.

Cecil held out a hand, like he was trying to calm a horse. He used a gentle tone. "Hey John, you don't have the training for this. You could really hurt yourself, and everyone else here. Why don't you put the chalk down, okay?"

John made one last addition to the circle and snapped the book closed. "It happens, you know. Someone without mage training becoming a gatekeeper. They even have a special spellcircle that's easier to work with. They call it merchant spellwork."

Al-Haythem leaned forward to examine the spellcircle. "That's true, but the contract for merchant-style gatekeeper contracts is more limited, so we don't usually use them."

John pointed with the chalk. "Right, exactly! But I'm not trained, so it's perfect for me."

Ahmet spoke up. "John, please put the chalk down, and step away from the spellcircle."

"Don't worry. I'm making you the heir," John muttered, eyebrows furrowed.

"That's not what I am worried about. You are going to blow us all up—or worse!"

John kneeled in the circle, closing his eyes as the chalk glowed. "Give me a moment."

The crowd backed away. Some even dove for cover, hands over their heads. Ahmet bolted for the door, but his foot got caught on the desk leg, and he half stumbled. Cecil took a step forward, but al-Haytham put a hand on his shoulder. "More dangerous to interrupt it at this point."

John raised his hand, pointing at Ahmet. "I name you my heir."

☙

Surrounded by infinite blackness, John's body glowed with a strange light. He hovered, surveying the area.

"Hello." A voice behind him spoke, and John whirled around.

"Husniye." John stared at the dead woman.

"You can think of this as a sort of memory I have bestowed upon you. A recording, if you would. So don't bother replying."

"A memory," John deadpanned.

"Yes, a memory. Now, I can't allow you to make anyone but Ece the heir. It would mess up too many of my plans."

John snorted, regarding the apparition.

"Now, now, no complaining. That's my final decision."

"I didn't say anything," John protested.

Husniye rolled her eyes. "How would I know that? This is just a memory, you know. Sent from the past. I can't hear you." She grinned slyly and winked. "Good luck. Keep one eye open while sleeping. Find Ece."

John woke up to see Cecil standing over him, worry and annoyance on his face. "You are the idiot," he grumbled.

"I saw Husniye."

"You want to go into details?"

"She said it was a memory, a recording. She said she couldn't allow me to make anyone but Ece the heir."

Ahmet came into John's view. "So it didn't work?"

John struggled to his feet. "I don't know."

Al-Haytham stroked his beard as he stared at Ahmet. "Sadly, it did not work. Olumtahss is still without an heir."

John brought his fist down on the desk. "Damn!"

Al-Haytham placed a hand on his shoulder. "It was a good spellcircle, though."

"Ece is the one missing, right?"

Al-Haytham nodded. "I am afraid so."

Ahmet cleared his throat. "Al-Haytham?"

"Yes?"

"Is it possible to clear the block that Husniye put in place?"

"Mmmm … possibly."

"Could you help John work on that? Preferably outside of my office?"

"Of course." Al-Haytham put a gentle hand on John's elbow and led him out of the room.

John and al-Haytham sat cross-legged on a magic circle in the basement, looking pained. Footsteps echoed down the hall, and Andrew of the Soissens Conglomerate walked in. "How is it going?"

Al-Haytham stroked his beard. He sounded as weary as John felt. "Husniye left a message for me on the stone. She told me to 'stop meddling.' It seems Olumtahss is further removed from the Spire contract system than originally thought."

Andrew breathed. "Ah."

John cocked his head. "When the Spire creates a gatestone, the rules for contracts and setting heirs is a fundamental part of the spellwork. Right? Husniye assured everyone that her stone also followed the rules."

Al-Haytham nodded. "Many times."

"So if she didn't follow the rules, why do I have to make Ece the heir? Why can't the gatestone do it?"

Al-Haytham clapped his hands. "Ah! Excellent question! Contracts aren't with the gatestones themselves but with the Spire. The gatestones simply act as a medium. Spire helps enforce them ..." Al-Haytham trailed off for a moment. "Well, they, hmm. There is an ... entity in the Spire. That is what you make the contracts with, and this entity expects things to work a certain way. Shenanigans will only anger the entity. That is the simplest way to put it."

"Who is the entity? Can I talk to them?"

"It's a golem, not actually alive."

"Then how does it get angry?" John accused.

Al-Haytham held up his hand. "I apologize. It's quite complicated, and I explained it badly. Husniye seems to have hijacked the contract system somehow, leaving us in our current predicament."

John clenched his jaw. "How?"

"If someone switched out a letter you sent, how would the receiver ever know?"

Without missing a beat, John replied, "The handwriting."

Al-Haytham grinned. "Very good. Basically, in this analogy, Husniye forged the handwriting. She was an extremely skilled spellworker."

John deflated. "Great."

Andrew frowned. "Is it possible to overwrite the spellwork somehow?"

"Of course. Give me a few months."

Andrew snapped, "We don't have a few months. You know that perfectly well, al-Haytham."

Al-Haytham offered a disarming smile. "The spellwork is very strong."

Andrew scowled at both. "It's also strengthened by having an active gatekeeper maintaining it, right?"

Al-Haytham didn't reply. After a few moments of silence, Andrew huffed and walked out.

John watched him go, and al-Haytham reached out to pat John's arm. "Andrew has an unfortunate tendency to blurt out things he shouldn't. It's gotten him in trouble before."

As Andrew's footsteps faded, John turned to face al-Haytham. "Do I have to be worried about anything?"

"Probably. They have no idea where Ece is, or even where to look, which is causing some desperation.

"You never really answered my question."

Al-Haytham raised his eyebrows. "Which one?"

"Why do we need to find Ece to make her the heir?"

"Ah. The contract requires both parties to be present."

"Can't we hijack it and change that?"

Al-Haytham gave a wry smile. "If I was as skilled as Husniye, maybe. But unfortunately, I am not. Interfacing with the Spire's spellwork should always be done carefully. They don't like games."

"Well, can we ask them?"

"To just remotely declare Ece the heir? To be honest, I don't know if that's even possible. Also, that assumes they would want to help."

"Why wouldn't they help?"

"If a month passes, the Spire gets the stone, remember?" al-Haytham said softly.

⌣

After the long day, and plagued by worries, John had trouble sleeping. The path forward was no longer clear.

He lay atop the covers of the bed, still dressed in unfamiliar clothes. Every ten minutes, he rose and paced the room, trying to figure out his next course of action. The rules and regulations he had read and memorized since arriving rattled around his head. "So one month.... And then ..." He tried to count the days that had already passed. The days blended together, but he was certain at least a week had passed.

"So now what?" he asked himself. There was no answer.

He lay back down on the too-soft bed. "What happens if the Spire takes the stone from House Husniye?" He couldn't shake the idea of people being harmed by the likely outcome.

At last, the world softened, and he drifted off to sleep.

He started at a barely perceptible click, then bolted upright. Cautiously, he rose from the bed and crept to the door. His hand hovered a half inch above the handle. "Anybody there?"

John waited, listening for the guard's reply. He grabbed the door handle and pulled the door. It swung open, hinges creaking. Someone had unlocked it.

The man waiting on the other side lunged at him.

John saw only a vague blob moving in the darkness, then his eye caught a glint of steel. He punched toward it, fist connecting with flesh. A yell, and the knife thumped against the floor.

John backed up, almost tripping over his own feet. More shadowy blobs strode into the room, fanning out. He grabbed a chair, raised it to throw, then hesitated. He spun, hurling it through the window instead. The expensive, flawless glass shattered.

He was on the fourth floor, too high to jump, but John didn't pause. He leaped through the window. He turned his body, reaching for the finger's width of window ledge above him. The tendons in his fingers and arms strained, but he held tight.

The assassin's feet pounded toward him as John pulled himself up to the window on the floor above. White hot pain lanced his leg as a knife grazed his shin. Then he was up, somehow, clutching the window ledge a floor above.

From there, he jumped to the wooden gutter, which creaked and groaned under his weight. A splinter pierced his palm, but he ignored the pain as he pulled himself onto the roof.

John stood. Taller structures enclosed this building, obscuring the horizon and cityscape.

He ran across the roof, then paused to get his bearings. Across the way, he spotted a bank of balconies. As he dashed that way, a hatch on the roof behind him crashed open. John glanced over his shoulder to see shadows emerging from the opening. John continued his sprint, ignoring their shouts, only to realize the gap was too wide to make the jump. Too late to turn around, John leaped off the edge of the building. He missed the first balcony but landed on the one below, the rail slamming into his chest.

He grasped the rail until he could breathe again, coughing painfully, then pulled himself up and over. He checked the door. Locked. He threw his shoulder into it. He bounced off as a crossbow bolt thudded into the wall next to him. Gritting his teeth, he stepped back over and began climbing down. His feet dangled, unable to reach the railing below. He kicked to find purchase. Another whistling sound next to his ear, another bolt barely missed. This convinced him to let go.

His feet hit the railing below, and for a moment it looked like he would make it. Then his balance shifted, and he fell backward. In a panic, he hooked a leg over the railing, then hung upside down. With a grunt, he pulled himself upright and onto the balcony. Wheezing, he reached for the door. This one was unlocked, and he burst into the room like a madman. Yanking open doors in search of an exit, he woke the apartment owners. Their groggy shouts growing louder, he finally found a door leading out of the apartment. He sprinted down the hall, found stairs, then bounded down them four at a time.

Once he reached the ground floor, the exit was obvious. He burst out onto the street. The night guard outside gaped at him. John paused to get his bearings, then pelted down the street, putting as much distance as possible between himself and House Husniye.

He raced down streets illuminated by mage lights, weaving around milling crowds of people chatting as they made their way home from bars. After a series of random turns, he ended up in a dimly lit back alley. His legs gave out. He collapsed against a wall, gasping for air. His whole body ached. As he sought to steady his breathing, John spotted a large, glowing sphere making its way down the alley. It paused, hovering. He forced himself to stand, then slipped back onto the main street.

He recognized this Spire City street. Taking a few deep breaths, he broke into a jog. After a few moments, he spotted the compound belonging to House Wu. The Chained Stone. John ran to the massive gate and threw his weight against it. A side door opened, and a curious head poked out.

John inhaled deeply and tried to keep his voice calm. "I need to get to Riverside." He didn't sound convincing.

"This is House Wu, not a public gate port."

"Where is a public gate port that can take me to Riverside?"

The man, bronze-skinned with a face covered with swirling tattoos reminiscent of rippling water, shrugged. "Is it a minor city? What continent?"

"It's south of the frostlands, to the west. The Islander Ocean. The coast."

"Oh, yeah, you'll want to head down that street until you see the statue, then take a right. It's the large building marked as Hub Three. What's the hurry?"

John was already jogging away. "Thank you!"

He soon saw the statue, a giant monolith holding a scepter. Its gaze cast at the giant spire in the center of the city. John took a hard right, not stopping to glance at the plaque at its base. As he ran, the architecture of the building shifted, becoming more familiar. The shingling turned red, the doors oaken, and the windows squared. A massive building, towering above all the others, came into view. A wooden veneer over the brick displayed intricate carvings, long since faded and cracked. John headed for it. The massive front gate was locked, but at a side door, a bored guard sat, reading something in the mage light.

"Riverside?" John asked.

The man looked up, unhappy with the interruption. "Yeah, but it's closed.

"It's a bit of an emergency."

"What's the emergency?" the guard asked.

"It's gatekeeper business." John held up the stone around his neck. "Is there a gatekeeper I could talk to? Or a mage?"

The guard pursed his lips, stared at the stone, and sighed the sigh of someone who wasn't paid enough. "You want me to wake up Charles?"

"That would be great." John nodded.

The man put down his book and waved at John to follow him into a foyer. "Wait there. I'll fetch him." The man pointed to a chair.

On the wall, John could see a sign indicating the direction of the Riverside Gatestone. "Actually, do you mind if I meet him there?" He didn't wait for a reply but moved through the foyer and deeper into the building, following the directions on the sign.

He passed massive domed hallways, with sunken cart tracks in the floor. Doors of differing sizes lined both sides of the wall. Some were enormous, decorated with a coat of arms and text below, indicating the gatestone destination. Smaller companion doors flanked each.

One of the large doors was open, and people pushed carts through. At the small door next to it, an armed guard glared at him as he strode past.

John stopped before a door painted with the image of a buck, blood dripping from its antlers. He knew this one: House Romanov, which ran the Riverside gatestone. He tried the door and found it locked.

"So who are you, really?" a voice behind him said. John turned slowly. An old man in his nightgown, white hair tousled from sleep, stood in the hallway. Behind him stood the guard from the front door. Wordlessly, John gripped the chain around his neck and held up the stone.

"Is that Olumtahss?"

John nodded.

The guard spoke up. "Charles, do you need me to stick around, or ...?"

The old man glanced down, and John saw him taking in a trail of blood where John had walked. He could now feel it running down his leg and into his shoe.

The old man didn't look away. "No, thank you," he said.

As the guard sauntered off, the old man regarded John. "I know who you are. There has been a bit of hubbub about you, sir. What are you doing here?"

"Please. I need to get to Riverside."

Charles sighed. "I don't want to get into trouble with House Husniye."

"I just want to get home."

"You are from Riverside?"

"I grew up there."

Crossing his arms, Charles stared him down. "What exactly is your plan?"

John met his gaze. "I don't want to die."

Charles blinked, exhaled. "That's not something anybody wants. All right, move it." He withdrew a giant ring of keys from nowhere. He flicked through them until he found the right one, then unlocked the door marked "Romanov." Inside was a massive red stone, shaped like a mountain. A circle of white tile flooring surrounded the gatestone. Metal tracks crossed the room, and a few old carts covered in flaking paint rested on them.

Charles directed John to step over the white line and up to the stone. "So, have you ever seen one of these before?"

John wondered if he was joking. "Yes. I saw the other side of this gate when I was a child."

"We used to use this all the time." Charles reverently placed a hand on the stone. "The church has, ah, clamped down on magic in the region. Now it's almost forgotten. All because of those Twisted." The man spat venom.

"If you don't want Twisted, why use Storm?"

Charles gave him a sidelong glance. "Why, indeed? Greed, I suppose. But that's man's prerogative, isn't it? Always pushing boundaries. Without greed, we would still be living in mud huts, would we not?"

"Greed seems to cause a lot of problems."

"It gives and takes. I say, let it give its gifts, but refuse to let it take anything in return." The old man gave John a toothless smile. "I suspect greed has brought you to me, and now I have the wonderful chance to tell it off and save a life. Good luck!"

～

When John made it to Riverside, he fell to all fours and dry heaved. Slowly, the world stopped spinning. Once he regained his senses, John warily glanced around the empty room, waiting for the sounds of footsteps or the creak of a door. None came. Sighing with relief, he crossed the room. He ignored the massive doors for wagons and carts and chose the one designed for foot traffic. It creaked with disuse. Walking down the dusty hallway, stepping around boxes in the faint mage light, he eventually found an unlocked exit door.

John stood in the street, and let his memories take him away. But only for a moment. Then he walked toward the poor part of town, toward the wharves where fishermen would haul in their catches for the day. The moonlight was barely bright enough to illuminate the dark street, and aside from the drunken revelers, the street was quiet.

John stopped in front of the inn, the only one with light on. The sign displayed a bed and bread. No words needed. Food and sleep—everything a man could need. John strode in. Luckily, someone was awake.

"I'll take a room."

The man on duty jumped. Narrowing his eyes at John, he asked, "What are you doing out so late?"

"Got kicked out."

The man pointed at a sign with a painting of two silver coins. "Two."

John patted where his money pouch would normally be, then paused, staring at the innkeeper.

The man blinked sleep from his eyes. "Do you have any coin on you?"

"No, sorry." John fidgeted with the buttons on his tunic. "Here, this is a nice tunic. You can have it as collateral."

"I'm not a pawn shop. You just want a bed for the night?"

"Please."

John struggled to stay upright as the man looked him up and down. "You look rough. We have an unused bed. Third floor, first room on the left is open. If you want sheets, I'll need coin."

John nodded in wordless thanks and headed upstairs. As he ascended, all the exhaustion and pain of the day hit him at once. He limped, leg aching from the knife wound. His chest throbbed, and his muscles felt like jelly. In the room, he took off his boots, then collapsed onto the hard bed. "I promised never to come back to this city," John murmured as he drifted off to sleep.

# 9

A man in ragged clothing knelt in front of Trey. They both eyed the stained rag on the desk. Chin in hand, Trey studied the cloth. "And you say this is his blood?"

The man nodded. "Oh yes, sir, they got him right in the leg, sir, yes, sir."

"Good job." Trey tossed a small, jingling pouch.

The skinny, hollow-eyed man, grabbed it midair, shot a toothless smile at Trey, and left.

A man sitting off to the side tittered. "Well, this is certainly interesting." He wore plain clothes, patched in several places, looking like an old street beggar. His shoes, however, were propped up on the table for all to see, gave away his wealth.

Trey gave the man a sidelong glance before sighing. "Don't you have things to be doing?"

The man grinned, all teeth and wide eyed. "I'm doing them." He wiggled his fingers like a puppet master. His laughter echoed unsettlingly.

Trey stood and plucked the rag from the desk. "Good. Stay here."

The warlock's smile was too large for his face.

Servants stepped aside as Trey strode the halls, eyes downcast. Without knocking, he entered an unadorned door. Inside were soldiers in the colors of House DuFort: deep-blue jackets with gleaming buttons, worn over white shirts and dark pants. They sprawled lazily around the room.

The soldier nearest the door nearly dropped his plate as Trey saluted briskly. "Sir!" The others jumped to their feet.

Trey waved them off. "I want you to get ready. Dress plainly. Meet me at the Seer Room."

Their captain stepped forward. "Yes, sir! No armor?"

Trey glared. He didn't recognize the man, so figured he must be new. "Nothing visible," he amended. He turned on his heel and exited swiftly. He heard the officer barking orders as he continued down the hallway, his feet clicking against the white marble floor. Now, he stopped before a deep-blue door with an eye engraved in the center, took a stone from his pocket, and placed it in the iris of the eye. At the click, Trey threw open the door and stepped inside.

The room was large and circular, with light gray walls that curved into a domed ceiling. The walls were polished to a mirror finish that reflected a single mage light hanging from a chain high above. In the center of the room lay a large slab of dark gray stone, with a dusky wood chair and a round table in the middle. Before the slab sat a few rows of wrought-iron chairs painted white. An ebony-skinned young woman in a white robe swept the floor.

Trey addressed her. "I want you to find someone."

She looked up, wide-eyed. "Sir, I'm just a trainee."

"Locate the hunter. The current gatekeeper of Olumtahss. I have some of his blood." He dropped the bloody rag on the table and sat in the wooden chair.

The woman froze, staring at him.

Trey cleared his throat. "This is an official request from the head of House DuFort to the seers." The woman nodded and, stumbling over her broom, scurried from the room.

As Trey made himself comfortable, another woman glided in. Her sky-blue robe trailed across the stone floor, her arms tucked in its sleeves. A loose hood enveloped her head, and a white veil hid her face. The veil hung haphazardly, as though it had been put on in haste. She gave a small bow, none of her skin visible. "We will need something belonging to the person you wish us to find."

Trey waved at the dirty rag. "His blood."

"Ah." the woman extended a hand, gloved in the same sky-blue as her robe. She held the rag between two fingers. "Sir? The gatestone he carries will protect him from seeking spells."

"I don't want excuses. Just do it."

"Very well, sir." At the front of the stone slab stood a white pedestal. The seer dropped the rag onto this, stepped back, and hummed softly. More veiled women trickled into the room, their robes whispering as they formed a semicircle around the pedestal. Their chant began—first as if each one recited different words. Suddenly, the sounds merged into one before diverging, then re-syncing, like many metronomes, each on a different beat.

Trey waited, his demeanor calm, as the sound grew.

A glow rose from the stone slab. The women's voices quieted, and the glow faded. Then the chanting surged again, the voices rising in volume, then falling, then rising again.

Behind Trey, several soldiers in plain clothing filed into the room, coming to attention as the strange chanting continued.

Finally, the stone shimmered. A faint face appeared in the air before him. Trey leaned toward the image. "That's not him!" he yelled. The chanting faltered, while some seers collapsed from fatigue.

"Probably a relative," a voice, raspy with age, spoke from the door.

Trey glanced over. "Matron," he barked, annoyed, "I didn't see you come in."

Though she wore the same sky-blue robe as the others, this woman had not troubled to veil herself. Her wrinkled face exuded calm. "If you had bothered to listen, you would know his stone protects him from seeking spells." Trey breathed heavily, his temper rising. He opened his mouth to speak, but she cut him off. "I can tell you one thing for sure; the hunter is in Riverside. Most likely taking shelter with his family there."

"And how would you know that?"

She glared at him, arms crossed. "I just finished breakfast with an old friend, who mentioned helping the hunter through the Riverside gate."

"I see." Trey glared at the matron, then turned to address the soldiers. "Go to Riverside. You saw the relative's face. You know the hunter's face. Find him. I have agents there. Use them if you have to."

"Sir!" The soldiers saluted and filed out of the room. Trey turned back to the matron, but she was already kneeling next to one of the collapsed seers, as white-robed women filed into the room carrying stretchers and medical supplies.

Trey turned to leave, but the matron interrupted him. "We are the seers of DuFort, not soldiers for you to order around. Next time you have a request, come to me first."

Trey clicked his tongue and stalked out of the room, slamming the door behind him.

In the absence of tapestries to dampen sound and add some color, Trey's footsteps echoed in the stone hall. It was always best to minimize the number of objects near a mage prisoner's cell. The stairs were arduous as always, and when he reached the top of the tower keep, he stopped to get his breathing under control. Before opening the door, Trey adjusted his clothes to make sure they hung well.

Outside the cell stood two guards, both wearing a small fortune in null-infused metal-plated armor. Behind the bars sat Ece, looking as infuriatingly serene as always. Despite her dirty dress, her sandstone-colored skin seemed to glow against the gray-blue stone of the cell. Without looking his way, she greeted him. "Hello Trey."

He glared down at her. "Ece."

"Here to do a little cleaning? These bars are looking a little dilapidated as of late."

The cell bars that had been polished to a mirror shine not long ago were coated with a layer of rust. Trey huffed. "Cute trick. I thought you should know that the hermit that Husniye threw her problems onto was just driven out of the house. They tried to kill him. Can you believe it?"

"Thank you for keeping me up to date on current events. Those two," she nodded at the guards, "aren't really talkative."

Trey felt himself flush. "That's all you have to say? Your house is doomed. I am going to rip it apart piece by piece, and when it's all said and done, you will either be dead or working for me."

"I like the dead option."

"I do hate wasting talent."

"And I hate talking to egotistical megalomaniacs."

Trey took a deep breath. "You may want to start cooperating. I am your only ticket to freedom. Nobody is going to be able to rescue you here."

"If my choice is between you or death, I'll go with death. Of course, the Spire will be quite annoyed that you killed a gifted gatekeeper.

"You do understand the situation you're in, right?" Trey's voice rose.

Ece smiled sweetly. "I do."

Trey turned on his heel and stomped away from the cell. Stopping in the doorway, he called over his shoulder to the guards. "Next time, I want to see her in rags." He descended the stairs with a smug grin on his face.

John stood in the center of inky black fog. He tried covering his eyes, but the darkness was still there, pulling at him. Faces formed in the air, pleading, making promises. John covered his ears, but he still heard a cacophony of voices deep in his mind.

"Enough!" he yelled in a voice that was both his and not his. Everything subsided for a moment, before coming back twofold. Vague shapes desperately tried to get his attention. "Is everyone here just trying to get something from me?"

He held up the bowl in front of him. "Give me something solid." The bowl filled with words and overflowed with promises. John sneered and threw it, scattering the words. "Nothing but empty promises and lies."

A moment later, John drifted into a deep sleep, dream free.

⌒

Cecil strode into the barracks, yelling, "Attention! Shakedown. I want everyone in a line."

The commotion was already in progress before he even finished speaking. Soldiers dropped hands of cards. Someone in the courtyard shouted for their sparring compatriots to get inside. Cecil waited, hands clasped behind him, back ramrod straight, as they gathered and stood to attention. "Where is Clinton?" he barked.

"His wife is sick, sir," one of the men responded.

Cecil nodded. "Recently there was an assassination ordered against one of our guests, John the Hunter. It failed. I want to know if anybody here was involved in it."

There was an uncomfortable silence.

"Nobody? Last chance to speak up." The silence continued.

Cecil visibly relaxed. "Well. Does anybody know who managed to completely fuck that up?" More silence.

"Did anybody notice the assassins as they prowled around the house? Or hear the commotion?" Nobody spoke up.

"Who was on night duty?"

"Sir, we were dismissed early."

"Dismissed?"

"Ahmet dismissed us, sir. Told us we were not needed that night."

Cecil stared off into the distance for a moment, jaw clenched. "Of course he did. Listen up, if Ahmet ever orders you to do something, let me know. I am not saying to disobey him but be sure to tell me immediately afterward. Wake me up if you have to."

The soldiers responded in unison. "Yes Sir!"

"Apologies for the interruption. Dismissed."

Cecil burst into Ahmet's room, startling the man's guests, who turned and stared at him. "May I speak to you a moment?"

Ahmet put a piece of paper on the table and stood with a grunt. "Captain Cecil." He nodded an apology to his guests and stepped toward Cecil.

Cecil met him halfway and hissed, "I liked him!"

"Cecil. Please."

"Why did you try to kill him?"

Ahmet responded slowly, as if addressing a child. "Because otherwise, he would have ended up giving the stone to the Spire. We don't know where Ece is."

"Oh, yes, and now we don't know where he is because you scared him off! The rest of the council is talking about …"

Cecil's volume was rising, so Ahmet cut him off. "Now is not the time."

"Then when is the time?" he replied through gritted teeth.

"Later."

Behind Ahmet, Cecil now saw representatives from House Romanov had gathered. He gave a small bow. "I apologize for my interruption."

A man smiled thinly. "It's fine, we were just discussing trade rights for opals."

Before Cecil could reply, Ahu came forward from a corner of the room, grabbed his arm—the one she knew was wounded—and dragged him back into the hall.

"Why are they discussing that without Beyzra present?" Cecil hissed.

Ahu sighed. In a whisper, she replied, "Trey submitted a request for the council to vote on the ownership of an unclaimed gatestone."

"There are no unclaimed gatestones."

"Trey found out John ran off, and Ahmet is running interference."

"It's not unclaimed. John has it."

Ahu patted Cecil's shoulder. "You know how these things go. As far as everyone is concerned, it's just a matter of time until it's unclaimed."

"Shit."

"For now, we still have the vote."

Cecil paced back and forth in the library. "Trey is talking to the rest of the council. He is trying to get them to promise to vote the gatestone to him if John dies without an heir. Ahmet is trying to bribe the council with whatever he can to keep the vote."

Al-Haytham watched Cecil pace above his reading glasses. "Does Trey know John can't set an heir?"

"I don't think so. All he seems to know is that John ran off."

"How did he find that out?"

Cecil shrugged. "Could have been anything! Any number of witnesses could have seen John running! Could have been one of the fucking assassins—" Cecil spat the word "—getting drunk at a bar and mentioning something! Who the fuck knows?" Cecil threw up his hands. "All I know is Ahmet may have just ruined us!"

"Well to be fair, if he did succeed in killing John, then the gatestone would have been back in our hands."

Cecil paused to stare out the window. "Right. And if he had gotten me and my men involved, maybe he would have succeeded!"

Al-Haytham smiled. "Would you have cooperated?"

"I wouldn't be happy about it, but he is currently acting head of House Husniye. I understand how the chain of command works."

"Technically, that's John."

"We all agreed that since he was an outsider, Ahmet would be acting head until it was passed to another member of House Husniye."

"We agreed to that, yes, but it is not in our charter. I'm just saying that Ahmet was probably worried about several things involving John. Of course, Husniye could have made it so even if John was dead, the only heir that could be set is Ece. There is no guarantee that having John dead will fix the problem. All it may have accomplished is to run out the clock for the month and the Spire to claim the stone."

Cecil sat down hard in a chair. "Why are you so calm about this?"

"Hmm. Nothing I can really do, I suppose. Have you tried contacting him?"

"John? He won't let me through."

"What were your intentions?"

"What?"

"Your intentions when you contacted him?"

"I wanted him to come back, I suppose."

Al-Haytham gave Cecil a small smile.

Cecil rolled his eyes. "Well, what should I be saying then? Hey, sorry my house tried to kill you?"

"That would be a start."

Cecil covered his face with a small groan. "Our gatestone, the stone this entire house was built around, is gone. It's. Gone. Husniye's legacy."

"Mmm. We still have the vote for now. If John were to die, we would still get Olumtahss, however helpful that would be. So obviously Ahmet will want John gone before Trey can flip the vote, yes?"

Cecil sat forward, focused "You say that like it's inevitable."

Al-Haytham shrugged. "I am sad to say, with Husniye's death, our political alliances have become far more … shaky. Romanov especially is … ah, how do I say this … wavering. I feel it's only a matter of time before Trey manages to convince him."

Cecil stood again. "Really? Really. And how will he do that? Vague promises of wealth? He doesn't have anything to offer House Romanov."

"Threats, I believe. Shutting down a gatestone. I know Blacktar City relies on them to transport food during the winter. Trey could shut that down."

Cecil waved a hand. "Doing that would ruin House DuFort! Trey would never do that!"

"He would, I believe. He is willing to burn down everything to get what he wants. That contract is extremely lucrative for DuFort, yes, but it is also necessary for House Romanov's survival. If Blacktar falls, then Romonov loses his seat of power."

Cecil stared at him for a second, then sank back into the chair. "Fuck. Trey would. He's crazy enough."

"Yes. And powerful enough to make threats. Husniye's death.... It was a powerful move."

"The Spire helped him. They hated Husniye."

"Obviously. But the question in many minds is how much was the Spire and how much of it was Trey? He has many convinced that the Spire merely offered ... scholarly support, and he did the rest. Many would bend the knee to ensure their safety."

Cecil pondered for a moment. "I'm not good at this sort of thing. I ... fuck. I wish Maria was here. I wish Ece was here." His voice wavered. "I wish Husniye was here." He took a few deep breaths.

Al-Haytham whispered, "Find Ece. That should be your priority."

"We have no idea where she is. Trey has us outmaneuvered on all fronts."

"He hasn't flipped the vote yet. Even if he does, he still has to kill John and bring the gatestone to the council. And John has proven to be tough. I also suspect if Ece was found, John would be more than willing to cooperate, simply to extract himself from this whole mess."

"Right. I guess … right. I'll get looking."

"Try Westport."

"Westport? Why would she ever go there?"

"Because she is human, Cecil." Al-Haytham smirked.

Cecil narrowed his eyes. "Are you … messing with me?"

Al-Haytham shook his head. "That's the only place they haven't really checked. They did some basic sweeps, but of course, why would one of Husniye's top mages ever need to go to Westport?"

# 10

John opened his eyes to find an unfamiliar ceiling. The sounds of a city filtered through the nearby window—clanging and banging, so different from the sounds around his cabin. With a grunt, he sat upright, winced, then rubbed his sore chest. Standing, he checked his pockets. All he had on him was his knife and a handkerchief. He'd slept well, somehow, and he was still alive.

He examined the room, then peeked outside. Someone already stood on the street below, hawking meat wares in the cool morning air. Making his way downstairs, he found the same desk attendant from the previous night on duty.

"Hey, thanks for last night."

The man waved sleepily at him. Steam rose from a mug in his hand. "Not a problem. We all have rough days."

As John stepped onto the street, memories blasted him. On his left, he recognized the spot he had once hidden to eat an entire pie he had stolen and made himself sick. Across the street was the old barbershop. Everything about the place was familiar, yet strange. John's head whipsawed from side to side as the city sprang to life. The bustle of the city unnerved him after he'd lived in the woods for so long.

Letting his legs guide him, he soon came to a large, ornate, circular stone temple. Familiar benches were arranged under the shelter of the portico, crude bedrolls resting on many. John reverently patted one bench as he passed. It was shorter than the others, and he was too long to lie on it now.

John knocked on the door and waited. A woman opened it, her white garb reflected the morning sunlight. He offered an awkward wave. "Ah, hello. Is Zen there?"

"She is. Who is asking?"

"Um. My name is John. I used to sleep on one of ..." He gestured toward the benches behind him. "I need some advice."

The woman smiled and nodded. "Come on, child." She offered John a seat inside and disappeared into the depths of the temple. As he waited, John fidgeted.

"John?" The woman who approached wore her hair, streaked with gray, pulled back in a bun. Despite her sun-wrinkled face, she possessed a charming, motherly look. She wore the white garb of the church.

"Hey, Zen."

She threw out her arms for a hug. "John! Come in, sit down, and let me get you some tea." She patted him affectionately on the shoulder.

A few minutes later, they sat in the kitchen, John listening to the clink of teacups. Unable to relax, he clenched and unclenched his jaw, fisted and unfisted his hands.

Zen set a hot cup of tea before him and took a seat across the table. "So."

"So," John replied.

"What have you been up to?"

John stared at the cup. "I took up hunting."

Her face fell. "John."

"I know. I ..." John started, then fell silent again.

Zen slurped her tea. "Well, are you back in town for good?"

"No. I ... well ..." John wordlessly took out the gatestone from inside his shirt and held it up.

She gasped, covering her mouth. "John, is that Storm?"

John sighed and nodded. "I ... Well, let me start from the beginning."

Upon finishing his tale, John leaned back. He had left out the part with the assassins, implying he fled House Husniye when the spell failed. "It's been a bit of a journey."

She grinned at him. "Well, that is an understatement if I ever heard one. I'll be honest with you, John, there were some days I was certain you were dead."

John looked sheepish. "Nah."

"I am glad to see you. Have you eaten?"

"No, not this morning."

"Let me get some food into you." She bustled about and soon set a bowl of soup and some bread before him. "Leftovers."

John picked up the spoon. "Thanks." He hesitated, then his question came out in a rush: "So this gem? I'm not going to turn into a Twisted, right?"

Zen gave him a knowing smile. "No, you are safe from that. As much as I dislike the Spire, their gatestones are quite safe. It's the rest of it that's ... bothersome."

John breathed a sigh of relief. "Right. Right. Okay."

"I'll be honest, I didn't know gatestones that small even existed."

John stared at the gem. "Neither did I." He took a deep breath, then blurted in a rush, "So, what's going on with my uncle?"

"He's alive, if that's what you are asking. Are you planning on visiting him?"

John didn't hesitate. "No."

Zen nodded. "Good. What's your plan?"

"I don't know. I was going to go back to the woods, hide out until the month passed, let the Spire claim it."

"It sounds like House Husniye won't be happy with that plan."

"No."

"I also noticed a nice gash on your leg. Does that have anything to do with you leaving House Husniye?"

John stared blankly at the ground.

Zen leaned forward. "John."

"I don't want to be a bother. Do you need any gardening done?"

Zen stood up "Come on, let's get you to the infirmary."

As she dressed his leg wound, John told her about the previous night. When he was done, she frowned. "Well, that's quite the escape. And you can't give the stone to anyone but Ece?"

"Exactly."

"If a month passes, the Spire has legal claim over the stone. If you die, the stone goes back to House Husniye."

"Yep."

She nodded. "The Spire is known to ... augment the natural rules of magic with rules of man. But rules of man can be broken, and rules of magic cannot. When the two are at odds with each other, things often end up Twisted."

John winced.

She gave him a smile. "Sorry, I slipped into preacher mode. Let me give you something." She moved to a cluttered shelf in one corner and rifled through knickknacks and random junk. After a moment, she returned, clutching something. She placed a jet-black rock on the table between them.

"It looks like an arrowhead," John said.

"It is an arrowhead. It's a nullstone arrowhead."

John's eyes snapped up to her, widening. "What?"

She waved her hand dismissively. "An old church relic. It was used to hunt down a warlock. Some long epic story."

"You can't give this to me."

She smiled. "Yes I can. I am the high priestess!"

"High? Since when?"

"Since the previous one died."

John motioned at her clothes. "Why aren't you wearing …?"

She gave John an impish smile. "I find it far too gaudy. Anyway, this is yours now."

"I can't accept this, Zen, I—"

She slapped the table so hard he jumped. "John, you are terrible at accepting help. I insist you accept this. There isn't much else I can do. You have been drawn into a dark place, and I can't pull you out of it. All I can do is insist you accept this, because I already failed you once, and I won't let you walk away without at least giving you something."

"Zen, you didn't fail me."

"That's kind of you to say, John. Now take the stone. And stay the night."

John stared at the nullstone for a few moments, sighed, then grabbed it. "Thanks, Zen."

~

Trey stared at the man cowering before him, dressed in the gaudy clothing only the poor thought looked expensive. "My name is Maxamillian DuFort the Third." The man stared until Trey prompted, "And you are?"

"Joseph. Where am I?"

Trey lounged in a chair, staring at the pudgy figure flanked by two well-armed men in the blue of House DuFort. Trey took a sip of his morning coffee, letting the man stew. "House DuFort. You don't look much like your nephew, John."

They didn't look much alike—John's face gaunt, his eyes deep set. Joseph's face was rounder, almost jolly.

After a moment's hesitation, Joseph asked, "So you know my nephew?"

"He has been causing me some problems. We know he is in Riverside. I would like you to talk to him. Of course, you will be compensated for your trouble."

Joseph, relaxed, grinned. "Ah yes, that little shit has caused me no end of problems, that's for sure."

Trey looked at him with hooded eyes. "John has something that rightfully belongs to me."

"Of course! That thieving bastard is always getting his hands on things that don't belong to him. I remember—"

Trey cut him off. "I need you to convince him to make a contract with me. To make me the heir. Can you do that?"

Joseph looked at him, confused.

With a thin veneer of patience over his annoyance, Trey continued. "I need you to convince him to make me the heir for the contract. Do you understand?"

"Ah, yes, of—"

"You will receive one full bag for your trouble. I want you to cooperate with my men who are already in Riverside, and I also want you to take this stone." Trey gestured at a fist-sized ornate, oval, blue stone on the table. "It's a seer anchor stone, and it will let me watch. Always keep it on you. Do you understand?"

Joseph nodded, then slowly lifted the stone and stuffed it into his pocket. "Yes, yes, of course, I understand."

Trey nodded at the two guards flanking Joseph. They grabbed Joseph by the arms and led him away.

Joseph struggled to turn around and wave as he was half dragged from the room. "Wonderful to work with you, sir!"

John walked through the busy morning marketplace, the coins Zen insisted he take with him jangling in his pouch. He didn't need much, just enough supplies to help him survive in the woods until the whole thing blew over. She had offered sanctuary at the church, but he had refused, not wanting to draw them into his current mess. He spotted a small bowyer shop and hoped it would have a bow that fit him well.

"John." Even in the din of the marketplace, John recognized the voice. He froze, one foot in midair, then turned.

"How are you doing?" John's uncle stood before him, arms open as if seeking a hug.

John's eyes went wide, and he took a step back. He was a child again, at his father's funeral, his uncle's hand on his shoulder like a steel vise. "I, uh …"

"I asked you how you're doing, John," his uncle repeated, letting his arms drop. Joseph wore an ornate leather jerkin over a long-sleeved shirt. His belt buckle shimmered, and the jewelry on his fingers gleamed. His necklace was a gaudy thing, all gold and gems.

John overlooked the empty gem sockets in his uncle's necklace and the crude repair job on his clothes. Nor did he see that he now stood taller than the other man. All John saw was the bully from his boyhood. He was breathless, barely able to get out a "Fine."

Joseph's smile didn't reach his eyes. "That's good to hear. Why don't we go have a drink together, we can catch up."

John gestured vaguely at the market. "I have to …, I have to …"

His uncle slid nearer to put a hand on John's back. "I've missed you, you know. We haven't seen each other in years. We really should catch up." He gestured toward a tavern with one hand, while pushing John toward it with the other, subtly nodding at one of Trey's plainclothes soldiers hovering in the mingling crowd.

"I have to go."

His uncle leaned close. "Listen, John, I have a spot open for you. It is your legacy, you know. Your father would be very disappointed to know you have not taken his place."

John's hand shook.

"I talked to Maximilian DuFort."

"Trey?" John whispered.

"Right. Trey." John's uncle sighed dramatically. "He told me about your situation. I'm sure we can figure out a solution that works for everyone. Now let's go talk about your future, right? Because you certainly can't keep doing what you are doing now." He pushed John's back again, harder. John took a single step forward, then stopped. "Look, John, things can go back to the way things were. Trey can make that happen. You remember the old house you grew up in? Not far from here? We can make that happen again. Don't you remember our maid? What was her name … Adaile? You remember that?"

John's heart beat so hard his temples pulsed.

"Relax, John. Everything's fine now. Just come with me, and we'll fix it. Together."

"I can't."

"Listen, John." Joseph put a hand on his arm, but John knocked it away.

"I fucking can't!" John shouted. He took a step backward, breath heaving.

His uncle screamed, "Will you stop acting like a child! What is wrong with you!" His face grew red. "What's your plan, John? What's your plan? Do you even have one? Or are you just going to run away again?"

"You always do this."

"Do what? Tell the truth? Rumor is that you have been living in the woods like a savage! What happened to everything your father taught you?"

"Fuck you."

"Answer my question. What have you been doing?"

"Fuck you."

"Stop acting like a child for once in your life! Please!" His uncle clasped his hands together and pressed them against his forehead. "I just want to help you."

For the first time, the two made eye contact. "You remember the iron?"

His uncle grimaced. "Is that what this is about? Is that what this is all about?" He threw up his arms in frustration. "Do you have any idea, any idea at all how hard it was to raise you? You are what is known as a problem child, John."

John's voice rose with every syllable. "You didn't raise me. You just dumped me on whoever would take me and then beat me when—"

The slap was loud enough to echo off the nearby buildings. "How dare you! I paid for your food! I paid for your maid! I paid for your bail! You remember that?"

John turned his gaze to the ground, eyes brimming with tears.

Joseph's voice softened. "What are you doing, John? You can't keep living like someone raised by wolves. Your father would have wanted more from you."

His voice barely audible, John said, "I can't."

Joseph thrust his face into John's, barking, "You little shit!"

"I can't make anyone the heir!" John screamed back. "Husniye did something! She made it so I can only make Ece the heir. I can only ..." John paused.

"What?"

⌒

Trey sat back in his chair with a sigh. The oracle stone before him shimmered in blue light, casting a pall around the room. The scene in the marketplace appeared on its smooth surface. "I guess we have to do it the hard way. Buying all those votes is going to be expensive."

He grabbed a carved, blue crystal from the table next to him and raised it to his mouth. "Kill him"

# 11

John's instincts screamed. He had just made himself expendable. By sheer luck, his darting eyes fell upon the man sauntering toward him with a knife in his hand.

He ran, recalling past years.

He pounded away from the market, moving down half-remembered streets, ignoring the stares of people he passed. He scanned the crowd, but the assassins were not visible. As he neared the stables, a flash of white caught his eye. He didn't question why Husniye's white horse was there, saddled and munching from a trough. John leaped on. The horse stopped eating, looked over its shoulder at him, then took off.

Behind him, John heard someone yell, "Stop, thief!" He thundered out of the city on white hooves.

When he had finally allowed the horse to nibble at some grass by the road, John sat upright in the saddle, wiped tears from his eyes, and took stock of his situation: He had the clothes he wore, his knife, the money Zen had given him, and the nullstone. He took it out of his pocket, thoughtfully rubbing it between his fingers. Pitch black.

John gripped the nullstone in his right hand and took the gatestone in his left, He hesitated, then slammed them together. Sparks flew, blinding John and burning his hand.

He blinked to clear the spots from his eyes. When he brushed his thumb across the surface of Olumtahss, he felt a small divot that rapidly disappeared, leaving behind a flawless surface again. He rubbed his hand, the sparks having left red marks. Horse craned his head at the disturbance, but continued grazing.

"Can this explode?" John asked Horse, who snorted and went back to eating grass. With a sigh, John returned the nullstone to his pocket.

The road ahead was winding and forested, leading away from the main trade thruway. Fallen trees and muddy puddles lay in their way. The horse's barrel turned brown as he forged through the deeper holes. John felt a sudden sensation, more a gentle nudge than the sharp headaches he'd felt before. This time, John didn't resist it. A voice came from the gatestone:

"John."

John's jaw tightened. "Cecil."

"I would like to apologize. If I had known ..." Cecil's voice trailed off. For a moment, John heard only the thump of the hooves. "They were afraid. If they lost the gatestone the entire house would collapse."

"Really."

"Well. It's complicated."

"I know."

"If you can't set an heir, it's a free-for-all. We can't protect you."

"Yeah. I figured."

A long, painful sigh came through the stone. Cecil's voice broke when he finally spoke. "I don't know what to do."

"Where's Ece?"

"We don't know. We can't find her. I'm going to check somewhere, Westport on Hydra Island, but it's a long shot."

"Find her and this is over."

"We think Trey has her."

John said nothing.

At last, Cecil continued. "I don't know what to do. If ... She raised me, John. Husniye did. I was an orphan; did you know that? She adopted me and raised me like her own child. And now she's dead. Everything she built, everything she worked toward is going to come undone. That stone is a symbol. It's really the only thing holding the house together." Another pause. "Trey is getting the rest of the Council of the Rose to agree to vote for him, so if you die, he gets the stone."

"Why would they do that?"

"Politics. He has a degree of legitimacy and the backing of the Spire. At least, he claims he does. If the Council of the Rose has a choice between the Spire or Trey getting Olumtahss, they would pick Trey. That would at least keep the stone in the council. It's very useful, gives them a major edge over the other councils."

"That's why House Husniye also tried to kill me."

"They tried to kill you to stop exactly this from happening. They're scared."

In a whisper, John admitted, "I'm fucking scared. I'm terrified. I don't know what to do. Why can't I just chuck this thing into a river?"

"If it's not on you, you can be tracked. You need to wear it to protect yourself, so don't take it off. If they find you, they will kill you to claim the stone."

John snapped, "So now you're giving advice."

Cecil's reply was calm. "Yes. I am. I won't lie to you. I'm an idiot, remember?"

John couldn't help the shaky laugh that ended in a sob. "Well, I guess I could use some advice."

"Stay on the backroads. Stay hidden. If we find Ece, I'll contact you, and we can bring her to you. You are already willing the stone to shield you, so just be careful not to let your guard down."

"Right."

"I'll find her. Trey couldn't have gone far."

"Trey has a gate network. He could have taken her to the edge of the world."

"Well ... yes."

"Good pep talk."

Cecil laughed. "My apologies. Honestly, I am not much for this sort of thing; Husniye always had a plan."

"Sounds like we could use her right now."

"I truly wish I could ask her for advice, just one last time. I'll be in touch."

"Right."

John let Horse trot forward, the rhythmic clop-clop calming his nerves. At a fork, John nudged it right, toward his home. Though it seemed obvious they would look for him there, John knew the woods. He could hide indefinitely. And the natural nullstone deposits should make it difficult to track him with magic.

As the shadows grew longer, John slumped forward in the saddle. By the time it grew dark enough that everything seemed to lose its color, he was nodding. When Horse stopped at a river crossing to drink, John dismounted. He removed the saddle and staggered from the road into a stand of trees, where he let it fall to the ground. Collapsing on a pile of leaves, John was asleep within seconds.

⌒

The dreamscape had changed somehow. The number of shadowy figures in the fog had increased, but they did not address him. They muttered to each other.

A woman strode forward, naked and beautiful, her hair and skin gleaming like the sun, her steps like a dance. John frowned. "Let me see your flaws."

She shifted into many forms, each as beautiful as the last—handsome men, gorgeous women, all enticing. John only repeated, "Let me see your flaws." With a silent scream, she melted into a puddle and dribbled away.

A splendorous figure walked in, covered in golden armor. He waved his hand, and piles of gems, precious metals, and carved stone statues sprang from the ground. He held a bag of gold out to John, who did not take it, but asked, "What is your purpose?" The figure gestured at the treasures. John asked again, and the figure faded away, like a sudden sunset.

A third figure approached, a merchant carrying a gigantic bag, stuffed to the brim. John asked, "What do you want?"

The merchant smiled a genuine smile, and said, "I have come to buy and sell, but mostly to experience the world."

John let him through.

⌣

"Good morning, sir."

John jolted upright, fumbling for his knife. A man sat nearby, skin dark as obsidian, smiling through white teeth. He looked well-traveled, with worn shoes and patches on his vibrant, patterned clothes. His voice was deep and melodious. "Sorry for startling you, but I must ask: Where am I?"

Breathing hard, John revealed his knife. "What?"

The man clicked his tongue. "Ah, I am sorry. I know you are new to this. I am an old friend of Husniye. You can call me Obi."

Slowly, John put the knife back into his belt. "Hello."

"Hello, Hunter. How are you doing?"

John hesitated before responding, "Terrible."

"Well, that is to be expected."

They sat in silence for a few minutes, John blinking sleep out of his eyes. Obi watched birds flitter around the trees.

"Uh, you are at the barrens. Outside of Riverside."

Obi nodded. "Quite full of life for such a name, isn't it? But the barren doesn't refer to the trees, of course. Now, would you like to trade?"

John blinked at him. "I don't have much."

"All the more reason to trade!"

John blurted, "I'm not giving you Horse."

Obi burst into a deep laugh. "Oh no, I wouldn't ask that of you. Snow is a treasure that cannot be traded."

"His name's Snow?"

"That's what Husniye called him. He's yours now, so you may call him what you want."

"Is he attached to Olumtahss?"

"Oh no, he chooses his rider."

John glanced at Horse, who was grazing. "I think I'll keep calling him Horse."

Obi laughed again, shaking his head.

Suddenly, John turned to Obi. "Have you ever heard of tree bellers?"

"The bird?" Obi asked.

"They are imbued, not natural."

"Cities are also not natural, yet we seem to love them so."

"Is Horse imbued?"

"He is, indeed."

John gave Obi a look. "What's the difference between an Imbued and a Twisted?"

Obi laughed, grinning widely. "The difference is mostly academic."

John stared at Horse, thinking.

Obi interrupted him. "So, what do you have to trade?"

"Nothing. I had to leave everything behind." John grimaced, realizing he shouldn't have said that.

Obi frowned. "Didn't have a chance to bring anything? Not even your bow?"

John looked away.

"Did you make it yourself?"

"Yeah."

"It's always sad to lose something you made with your own hands. There is something special about it that cannot be replaced. It is much easier, and yet harder, to forgive its flaws when it's your hands that made them."

John mulled those words. "What do you want?"

"Honestly, I was hoping you would be somewhere livelier. Husniye always went to the most interesting places. Traveled the world, she did, even to places far from gatestones, to the wild lands. Not as wild as one would think, of course. I also wished to meet you, the heir to the stone."

"Well, hello."

Obi laughed again. "Ah, don't be so hard on yourself. Husniye chose you, and she doesn't do things without a reason."

"She chose me because I happened to be the only one around."

"After she was attacked?"

"Yeah."

"And you know where she was attacked?"

"Near me?"

Obi shook his head.

John began, "I just assumed …".

"Assuming things with Husniye is generally a poor decision. It ends badly for everyone involved, yes?"

John furrowed his brows. "I never met her before. Why did she come to me? How would she even know?"

"Ahh,… I told a half-truth. Or a complete truth, but only part of it. She could not go very far,… well, I suppose it would be far for you, yes? A few days of travel at least. And yet she ended up on your doorstep."

"Why me?"

"That's my question."

"I don't know."

Obi flashed his white teeth. "It is so much harder to examine the self. After all, there is no mirror for the soul." He clapped his hands together. "So. Time to trade." He unslung his backpack and placed it in front of him, a ratty old thing held together with stitches and patches, various bits and bobs tinkled as it moved.

"I don't have anything."

"I will settle for a story," Obi said with a smile.

"Really. In exchange for what?"

"You needed a bow, did you not?"

John stared at Obi incredulously. "You'll give me a bow in exchange for a story?"

"Perhaps. One about yourself. An important one."

"Why?"

"Information is king and can be worth far more than any chunk of wood. Besides, I may not look it, but I am quite rich." Obi reached into his backpack and pulled out a gold bar. John's eyes widened. "So for me, I think it would be a fair trade." He dropped the gold bar back in his pack.

"Was that real?"

"Heavy enough to be real. Would you like to feel it?"

"It's fine. So you are an information broker, then?"

"Among other things." Obi waited as John sat deep in thought before finally settling into a more comfortable position.

"I'll tell you the story of the first time I killed a man."

"I was walking down an old, dusty road. The day was hot and sticky, and my skin crawled with sweat. I was young, too young, to grow a real beard, though I tried many times. My leg ached. My dad had died, and my uncle Joseph took over the family business. He had punished me for something. Don't even remember what, but it hurt to walk.

"So I stopped under a tree. I'll be honest, I hadn't really done much planning, didn't even have any water. I ended up eventually going back, staying at the Storm Church, doing odd jobs for a year or two before I struck out on my own. Anyway, I was under this tree, resting, and I think I may have even fallen asleep when this man startled me. Wanted to know where I was going. I found out there were three of them."

John paused, and Obi waited for him to continue.

"I remember how skinny they were. And the scars on their forearms, the kind you get from being in a knife fight, you know what I mean?"

"Oh yes, of course."

"They wanted to know where I was going, so I made up something. I think I said I was going to meet my dad. I don't remember. They didn't buy it and started asking questions. You know that feeling when something is wrong, but you can't put your finger on it? That fear in your gut, even though they haven't done anything. They offered to give me a ride, but I turned them down. They insisted. One tried to grab me. I kept the tree between us, ducking and weaving around, staying out of his reach. His friends were laughing, and he got frustrated. Pulled out a knife, a big one. I had a knife too, but it was a small thing.

151

His friends laughed even harder when they saw it. The guy swung a little too hard, and the knife got stuck in the tree, so I tried to cut his arm. At the same time, he pulled the knife out and went for my throat. As luck would have it, my knife hit his, and his was cheap, so it broke. Then I stabbed him and ran."

John picked up a stick and traced patterns into the dirt in front of him. "I found out later I killed him. They weren't good men."

Obi nodded. "Quite the story. A good choice. Exciting, but doesn't give away too much about yourself. Except your powerful will and desire to live."

John glared at Obi. "Do you even have a bow?"

Obi reached into his bag, pulling out a long stave of beautiful white wood, a bit thicker than a fist. Where light hit it, the grain glinted like gold.

John studied the length of the stave, then the size of the backpack. "How?"

"This is angelwood. Very durable, rare, hard to find. Straight grain too." Obi rotated it from one end to the other so John could see it was the core of a tree. "No knots, a perfect stave. Not a bow yet, but I suspect you would rather make it yourself."

"What I want isn't important. I don't have time to hunt right now. I need to move fast. I need food."

"Of course, of course. Food for another story. And let's up the ante. Something about yourself this time."

John narrowed his eyes. "So you can sell it."

"Perhaps."

John listened to the morning birds. He took a deep breath, let it out, and began. "She was pretty. I remember that much, though I can't picture her face anymore. I do remember her name: Naisha. Cute accent too. She was our maid, about my age. This was before I tried to run away.

"Two teenagers under the same roof, you can imagine what happened. That night I was just waiting for her to finish the dishes. In hindsight, I could have helped her, so the dishes would be done faster. But that seemed rude since that was her job. Sorry, I'm rambling.

"I remember she smiled at me like she always did. After she finished, she grabbed my hand and led me upstairs to my bedroom." John scratched vigorously at the dirt. "I have had a lot of time to think about it. Something about it doesn't add up, because we didn't hear him come up the stairs, and they were creaky. Anyway, my uncle burst into the room, screaming. We scrambled to cover ourselves. He was upset I was sleeping with the maid, sullying the family name, you know. On and on. Looking back, it sounded like a prepared speech.

"I was flippant about it. I shouldn't have mouthed back, but I didn't know how … bad he could be. And now I wonder, why hire a woman my age to be our live-in maid? He would do shit like that, set you up to fail so he had an excuse to go after you. Asshole." John jabbed at the ground with the stick. "Anyway, I was mouthing off at him, and he ordered me out of the room. I stormed off. I should have stayed or taken her with me." John wiped his eyes.

"I could hear their voices. At first my uncle's tone was lecturing. But Naisha had some fire in her. I could tell she wasn't saying what he wanted to hear. He got angrier and angrier. Then she started screaming. I rushed back in. There was a lot of blood. We had an old carpet, and he rolled her up. He was saying that if anyone found out, they would take the business and my father's legacy would be gone, so I had to help. I was scared. We carried her downstairs in the carpet; he bribed ..." John's throat closed. He swallowed. "After, he lectured me more. I don't remember it. I never forgave him either...." John trailed off.

Obi gave him a sad look. "Your first love?"

"Yeah."

Softly, he continued, "Your only love?"

John looked away.

"You seem to be a man stuck in the past."

"Thanks, very helpful," John grunted.

Obi gave him a gentle smile. "Good! Glad I could help! But really. You'll be fine."

"How. How will I be fine?"

"Because you are still alive. Despite all odds. Someone hard to kill is someone who eventually wins," Obi replied.

Horse nudged John's shoulder. John hesitated, then patted Horse on the head.

Grinning, Obi stood. "Well, you covered your end of the bargain, I suppose. I will fulfill mine." He placed the stave on the ground, then upended his bag. A cascade of food fell out: Sausages, bags of flour, pots of oil, and fruits, followed by a canteen. Obi shook the bag again, and a leather bag plopped on top of the pile. One more shake and a few whetstones fell out, along with a small whittling knife. "Good luck!" Obi said and then he was gone.

# 12

Cecil walked down the road. The air smelled of seawater and horseshit, and the sandstone houses shone in the bright sun. Up ahead, Westport, which the sailors called Whoresport, loomed—a town of privacy curtains, drinks, and all the pleasure one could buy.

He grumbled, "There is no way Ece would ever come anywhere near here." But al-Haytham had a point. House Husniye agents had only conducted a cursory search of the island. The local authorities had pitched in, but Westport was known for keeping its visitors' secrets. If Ece had indulged, confirming so would have been difficult. He looked around the busy street. "Where do I even start?"

Before long he found what he was looking for—a public house serving food. As he entered, he called out, "What's today's dish?"

The burly, middle-aged woman behind the counter pointed at a pot bubbling over a small pile of coals. "Fish soup." Cecil dropped a coin on the counter. She inspected it, then ladled a healthy serving into a wooden bowl. "Bring that bowl back when you are done," she mumbled.

He chose a table outside. The soup smelled good, at least. He sat for a while, eating and watching the other diners. One woman caught Cecil's eye. She sat alone in the sunlight, tan skin and black, curly hair pulled into a messy ponytail. She was beautiful. He waited to approach until she had finished her lunch.

"Excuse me, ma'am, I was wondering if you could help me out with something."

She startled, looking up. "Uhmm …"

He held up an image of Ece etched into a stone tablet. "My sister has gone missing, and I was wondering if you had seen her."

The woman considered the likeness, then glanced back at him. "No, sorry, I don't recognize her."

Setting the etching on the table, Cecil took the seat across from her. "I don't even know where to start looking for her around here."

Studying the image again, the woman frowned, saying, "She doesn't look much like you."

"Adopted sister. We grew up together. She went missing not too long ago."

"I'm sorry."

Cecil gave her a sly smile. "Well, if you don't mind me asking, are there any brothels here that specialize in serving women?" Seeing her expression, he added, "Not that I'm implying you … partake. A woman as beautiful as you should never need to pay for …." He trailed off, glancing sideways at her.

Her blush was visible despite her tanned skin. Her gaze dropped to her lap. "There is a place, um, at the north end. The Fisherman's Pole."

Cecil gave his most charming smile. "I don't know this island very well. If you don't mind, I would love it if you could walk me there."

Suddenly a shadow loomed over them, and Cecil glanced up to find the burly cook, who was glaring at him, arms crossed.

Cecil raised his hands, "Ma'am, you don't need to rescue her from me. I assure you I don't bite. I was just asking about my missing sister." He gestured at the etching.

She glanced down. "I recognize her."

Cecil's head snapped up. "What?"

"She ate here with her girlfriend a couple of times."

"Girlfriend? As in, a friend who is also a girl?"

"Didn't seem that way to me." She laughed as Cecil's mouth rounded into a big O.

"That explains so much!"

The beautiful woman across from him gave a muffled snort.

"Do you remember anything else?"

The burly woman shook her head. "No, sorry. I just remember her face. Didn't even catch their names."

"What did the girlfriend look like?"

"Pretty. A local."

"It's not you, is it?" quizzed Cecil.

She smirked. "No."

"Well, at least it's a lead. Wait, you said a couple of times?"

"Yeah."

Cecil stood, bowed, and thanked the women. Eyeing the beautiful woman, he said, "My name is Cecil. Would you like to join me for drinks? You could help me brainstorm where to look for my sister."

"I think I'll have to turn you down."

"Already taken?"

She nodded.

"Well, he's a lucky guy. Or girl," Cecil added. "Oh well, can't blame a guy for trying."

Cecil walked away. Al-Haythem had been right. Ece had been on Hydra Island. He needed to find a communication stone, fast.

He found a spot almost immediately. Despite its size, the island held many spellstones.

Al-Haythem's voice echoed around the stone room. "A cornerstone of Hydra Island's business model is its safety. This high-profile kidnapping would be a blemish on their reputation. When our representatives asked, they said she hadn't been here. But then again, privacy is another key to their business."

"She never mentioned coming to Westport to me. Did she say anything to you?"

"No, never outright, but I suspected."

"I mean, I wouldn't have judged her," Cecil sputtered.

"In your case, I don't think it was fear of judgment. A conversation comes to mind, whereupon she said that if you ever visited Hydra Island, it would be like unleashing a fox into a henhouse."

Cecil paused. "She stole my date! During the ball! Oh, I am going to have to give her shit for that."

"Cecil, focus! Last time, we sent a team in Husniye colors. Everything official and above board. Clearly, the official visit had difficulty bearing fruit."

"Sounds diplomatic and annoying anyway. I'm not the best at that sort of thing."

"Perhaps you should play to your strengths then? Do you need any assistance?" al-Haytham asked.

Cecil pursed his lips. "Not right now."

"I'll let you get back to it."

"Ah, one thing, al-Haytham. Do you think Ece was embarrassed by me?"

Al-Haytham chuckled. "Only when other women were involved."

Cecil's shoulders slumped. "Ah. Right. I'll let you know if I find anything." Al-Haytham cut the connection. Leaning back in the chair, Cecil glanced at the gatekeeper. "How much?"

He indicated a large wall sign. "Five minutes is ten."

Whistling, Cecil dropped a large coin on the table. "A day's wage? Here you go." Standing, he pulled out a second large coin and held it up. "If anyone asks, I was just talking about the quality of the whores here."

The man pocketed this coin. He dropped the other in a box. "Of course, sir."

Cecil stepped out of the room, closing the door behind him. A desk clerk called "Next, Red Flower Room" to the person standing at the front of the long line in the hall. Cecil strode past, out of the building, and back into the sun.

Cecil returned to the street, sword at his side. Other than the occasional bodyguard, most people on Westport went unarmed, so he drew a few glances as he walked. Suddenly, ahead, he spotted a man in a white mask, walking with three collared servants in tow. Cecil stopped. "A White Mask?" he whispered.

A tapping sound came from Cecil's right, an older gentleman with a cane. "Yup," the man said, scowling at the masked man from underneath his hat. He rapped his cane against the ground again. His accent identified him as a local.

"I didn't know they allowed collared prostitutes here," Cecil replied. "Isn't that a security risk?"

The old grumbled. "They don't. They are only allowed to sell 'em. They're supposed to stay in their enclave too."

"Hmm, that makes sense. There are a lot of rich clientele around here."

The old man spat. "Never know when those things are going to pop off and start stabbing people. Gives me the creeps. They should outlaw them." He tapped his cane for emphasis.

Behind them, someone scoffed. "They don't 'pop off.' They are perfectly safe."

Cecil glanced back to see a pale young man with a purple scarf around his neck and striking black clothing, a sneer on his face.

The old man wheeled around. "That ain't what I heard. Haven't you heard of the murder of Countess Daphne? They say her own collared slit her throat in the middle of the street."

"You just believe everything you hear, then?"

Cecil stepped between them. "I am not defending the practice, but well-made collared will always do what their master says." He silenced the elder gentleman with a gesture, then addressed the younger. "The problem is that they aren't perfect at telling who's their master and who's not."

The purple-scarfed youth crossed his arms. "The spellwork takes care of that."

"Everyone always thinks their spellwork is perfect, but it rarely is," Cecil retorted.

The youth threw up his hands. "They are tools. If you are stabbed with a stolen knife, you don't blame the owner of the knife, you blame the person who stabbed you."

The old man tapped his cane again. "Tools can't chase you down the street."

"Waste of my time," the youth said with a scoff.

Cecil watched him go, then held up the image of Ece. "While I have you, have you seen this girl?"

The man shook his head. "Friend of yours?"

"Adopted sister. She went missing."

"I'm sure she's fine."

Cecil scratched his ear. "Do you ever see collared without an escort?"

"Of course, lazy nobles always send them to do their errands. They ain't supposed to, but nobody stops 'em." He patted Cecil on the shoulder. "If you are worried a White Mask grabbed your sister, they only go after criminals, outlanders, and wildmen. I wouldn't worry about it."

Cecil gave him a strained smile. "Right. Thanks. Thanks for your time."

"Good luck on your search,"

Cecil turned away but then turned back. "Ah, one more thing. Do you know anywhere around here I can get a good map of this island?"

"Two blocks that way, turn left, two more blocks. On your right."

"Thank you, good sir. Have a nice day."

Cecil grimaced at the expensive map. The intended clientele was obvious: the brothels were clearly marked. Cecil had circled those closest to the public house where Ece had been seen.

Near the wharf, sailors loitered. Before several buildings, burly armed guards stood watch, prepared to handle anyone who got drunk and disorderly.

Cecil watched the chaos for a moment. A man wearing a long scarf walked past with a bag, the scarf slipped to reveal a slave collar—property of the White Masks. Ahead of him, a man dressed in sailor's clothes ducked into a whorehouse. One glance at the shoes told Cecil they were too expensive for any sailor. He grunted thoughtfully. A group of four lingered nearby, wearing loose tunics and head wraps to shield them from the sun. They eyed him with interest, so he stepped that way.

"Evening, gentlemen. I was wondering if you could help me with something."

One smirked. "You lost?" Another laughed.

Cecil grinned back. "I was wondering if you could point me to an information broker around here."

"What makes you think we would know anything about that?"

Cecil pointed at the man's forearms. "Nice scars. Get those from sailing?"

"Fuck off."

Cecil pressed in. "No tan lines, either. Always sail on overcast days?"

The man frowned. "I don't get tan lines."

Cecil rested his hand on his sword. "Really?"

A third man, with much darker skin, gestured at the group. "Runs in the family. We're brothers, see?"

Their differences were stark. Cecil snorted. "Sure you are."

"You have no right to tell someone who is and isn't their family." The scarred man crossed his arms, and the other three shifted to form a half-circle around Cecil.

Cecil took a deep breath and removed his hand from his sword. "Maybe we got off on the wrong foot. I am looking for my sister. She likes to … find companionship in Westport. Instead of walking all over the city, I figured some enterprising individual probably keeps tabs on that. I would like to purchase this information. Does that make sense to you?"

The third man laughed. "Your sister was visiting whorehouses? If she needs a man, I would be willing to …"

Cecil slid his sword out of the scabbard in one smooth motion, and the man took a step back. "Hey. We are just playing."

Cecil clenched his jaw and slid the sword back into the scabbard. "Sorry, I have had a long day. Getting a little cranky."

The four men huddled up, talked among themselves, and glanced at Cecil. Finally, one broke away and stepped forward, holding out his hand. Cecil dropped a generous pile of coins into it. The man with missing teeth grinned.

"Down that way, take a right, then another right. On your left, it's the building with a big oak door and circular windows. Good luck, fellow." He gave Cecil a small sarcastic bow and the group absconded with their new wealth. Cecil grunted, then walked away.

At the rich oak door, Cecil knocked. A hatch slid open. Two eyes, barely illuminated by the fading sun, peered back at him. "You know," Cecil remarked, "bolting this nice oak door into sandstone seems like quite the waste. It would be pretty easy to just pull it off."

"What do you want?" the voice growled.

"Information on Ece Husniye."

"A moment." The hatch slid shut. Cecil heard a muffled shout. "He's asking about a Husniye!" More muffled voices, and then the hatch slid open again. Another pair of eyes peered at him for a second, then disappeared. More muffled talking. Finally, a third pair of eyes. "What do you want?"

"Information on Ece Husniye."

"We don't know anything."

Cecil fingered his coins. "Name your price."

"We don't know anything."

"I don't believe you."

"Well, sorry you feel that way." The hatch slammed shut.

Cecil pounded the door, yelling, "I don't have time for this. I can pay. Let us do business." But there was no response, so Cecil reached into his coat and pulled out a small, white stone covered in intricate carvings. He pressed his ear to the door. Someone was still there. He held up the stone. "I'd hate to use this flashstone. This is a really nice door."

Quickly, the door opened. A short man with salt-and-pepper hair and heavy jowls stood in the doorway. Reading glasses perched on his hook nose. A well-groomed goatee lined his face, and his clothes were well fitted and solid. He wore no jewelry, only the weary expression of an old person dealing with the exuberance of youth. "There are certain ways things work in this world. You can't throw a tantrum and expect to just get what you want. Running around and saying you have a flashstone is a good way to die. Just some friendly advice from someone who has been doing this a long time, all right? Now please, go home."

Cecil raised his hand and pointed down the street, muttering. A flash and explosion followed. Surprised yells echoed nearby.

Before Cecil could react, the old man ducked back into the building and slammed the door. Through the hatch, he yelled, "Are you fucking crazy!"

Cecil dropped the now useless stone on the ground as it shattered into dust, then reached into his pocket and pulled out another one. "Let me explain something to you. Ece, someone who I consider my sister, has been kidnapped. I am willing to burn this entire island down to find her. All I want is some information, and I am willing to pay well for it. So why don't we all just cooperate before I really lose my temper?"

"You should leave."

Cecil sensed the two men approaching from behind before he heard them. He sighed. "Fine. We'll do it the hard way." Cecil pocketed the flashstone and pulled his sword out as he turned to face the new threat. The two men possessed knives and arm braces but little other weaponry or armor.

The old man's voice came through the hatch. "What do you think you are doing?"

Squaring off, Cecil yelled over his shoulder, "Getting answers. Where is she?"

Seizing the opportunity, the first man lunged at Cecil. Without missing a beat, Cecil sidestepped and flicked his sword to the side, catching the man in the throat. He dropped the knife and fell, gurgling. The second man dropped his knife and signaled surrender. Cecil took a step back, and the second man rushed forward to help his friend stand. Both retreated, the second one dragging his friend and insisting, "You'll be fine. Don't worry! I'm sure you'll be fine."

Cecil turned back to the door. He held the second flashstone at the open hatch. This time, a voice from the hatch gave him instructions.

"Go to the Tattered Blouse. We know Ece visited it."

"Thank you. If you are lying, I will find you and kill you. Have a good day."

The sun had set when Cecil arrived at the Tattered Blouse, but the streets were busier than ever. Expensive mage light street lamps illuminated the road behind him. This block, however, was lined with cheaper, dimmer oil lamps. The clientele here wasn't as wealthy as those in the center of the curtain district. Arriving at the Tattered Blouse, Cecil pushed the red curtain aside. Inside smelled of piss and cheap beer, and the floor was stained. A woman greeted him with a smile. She wore too much makeup and a corset that had seen better days.

She smiled at Cecil with missing teeth and horrid breath. "Who you looking for, hon?"

Cecil held out the slate with Ece's image. "My sister has visited this place. Know anything about it?"

The woman twitched. "You had best leave, I think."

Cecil grinned like a wolf who had just found a fresh carcass. "Did you hear that loud boom earlier?"

Her eyes widened, and she bolted into the next room, shrieking "Jen! The explosion guy! He's here!"

"Well, news travels fast here." He followed her through the door and was greeted by a chorus of screams. He stepped to one side as a large woman charged him. She missed and went sprawling with a yelp. Cecil held up his sister's image. "I'm just here for information. Have you seen this woman?"

Many women huddled against the far wall, terrified. But a petite blonde in a revealing white dress stepped forward. She gave him a teasing smile. "The woman in that picture doesn't work here. But if you want something, anything at all, feel free to let me know and I'll try to make it happen, okay, big boy?"

Cecil was exasperated. "Listen. Ece was like a sister to me. You are going to tell me what I want to know, or I am going to raise hell."

"Wait. What's your name?"

Cecil hesitated before replying, "Cecil. Why?"

She made a face. "Oohh." Behind her, the other women relaxed. "Ece did mention you." The blonde woman introduced herself as Candy, and in short order, the women had him seated comfortably with a drink in his hand.

"So she was dating a woman named Yeela?" Cecil asked Candy.

"Yep, two regular old lovebirds. Pretty damn romantic, ya know? One a princess, the other a poor orphan from the street, just trying to make her way ..." Candy gave a wistful sigh. "They had a big falling out though. Yeela wanted to get out of this life. Get a job at House Husniye. Ece refused."

An unpleasant thought occurred to Cecil. "When Ece disappeared, did Yeela end up with a bunch of money?"

The three girls were quiet. The woman from the front room, the one with the missing teeth, whispered, "Yeela disappeared too."

Cecil rubbed his forehead. "What? Shit. What happened?"

There was another awkward silence, before the large woman blurted out, "Someone saw some collared grab her."

"Bertha!" Candy exclaimed.

Bertha made a face. "He deserved to know."

Cecil leaned forward. "Their master's crest is usually embedded on the collar, at the front. Did they see the crest?"

"I can tell you they were probably unsold. Worked directly for the Masks. We have seen them around before. They kidnap girls sometimes, especially troublemakers, and Yeela had an attitude problem."

Cecil tugged on his sleeve. "Where did Ece and Yeela usually meet up?"

"Here at first," Candy said, "But then they started using some spellstone to arrange meetings. Yeela showed it to me. Ece gave it to her as a gift."

"Is there anything else?"

"Not really."

Cecil dropped a few coins on the table. "For your trouble. Thank you for the help."

Bertha swept the money in one big palm, while Candy rose to show him out. "Good luck."

# 13

A sliver of wood joined the pile on the ground. John slid his hand up the bow, feeling every imperfection, then, ran the blade along it again. Another small slice of wood fluttered to the ground. Beside him, a campfire's embers glowed, a flat rock sizzled at the center. Next to him sat another flat rock with a single piece of flatbread on it. It was the last of a large batch he had made with flour and water fried in oil. Hunger and abundant supplies had driven him to make more than he needed, but the flatbread would keep for a day, so it wasn't anything to worry about.

Patting the wood with one hand, John raised the other to his mouth and took another bite of the sweet fruit Obi had left, one he had never seen before. He leaned back, putting his foot on the center of his rapidly forming bow, gripped the two vines he had tied to the ends, and pulled. The parts bent into a large arc, almost even. Gradually, John released the vines, allowing the bow to unbend, then picked up his knife. A careful stroke removed another sliver of wood. The gurgling of the creek nearby kept him company as the sun raced across the sky.

Night came, and John slept under the stars as wisps of cloud moved across the sky. In the morning, John ignored his aching hands and went back to work as the bow continued to emerge from the wood.

⌣

John and Horse drew many stares as he approached the market. He suddenly wished he matched the horse better. Horse's embroidered saddle and harness stood out compared to his current state. When he dismounted, the villagers pretended to busy themselves.

John fumbled for a moment before placing his new bow, still stiff, on the counter. He grinned at the merchant, reached into his bag, retrieved a jar, placed it on the counter with a quiet thump.

The merchant looked at the jar, then back at John. "What is that?"

"Oil. I'm selling it."

The merchant unstopped it and sniffed. He maintained a neutral expression even as he realized the quality of the aroma. "What price are you asking?" the man asked.

John nodded toward his new bow. "Bowstring and arrows. For this."

"And?"

"A few good steel broadheads would be nice. But I could mostly use bodkins. Hardened." Hardened steel bodkin arrowheads penetrated armor. Man-killing arrows. Owning them was discouraged.

The merchant frowned. "Hardened steel bodkin arrowheads. I don't have any of those."

"Bullshit."

There was a moment of silence as the merchant glanced at Horse, whose head and shoulders blocked the doorway, and then back to John. "Okay. I can give you ten, but I don't know if the length is right for that bow."

"Bowstring first."

The merchant grabbed the jar of expensive oil and placed it behind the counter. With a thoughtful expression, he opened a box and handed John a sturdy wax-covered string.

John quickly tied two loops and put one over one end of the bow. He then put the bow between his legs, bent it, and slipped the second loop onto the other end. He pulled back the string, grinning wildly. "Arrow." He held out his hand.

The merchant passed John an arrow. "Blunt tip, but it's the same weight and length as the bodkin." He cast a worried look at John. "There is a target set up down the road there, feel free to try."

"Thanks." John interrupted, spinning away from the merchant and drawing back the arrow. Horse's head disappeared from the doorway.

The merchant gasped, "Uh. You …"

The arrow flew true. It thunked into the lintel of the house across the street, frightening a passerby, who jumped and almost dropped the dead chicken he was carrying.

"Are you insane?" the man shouted.

John crossed the street to retrieve his arrow. He grunted and yanked the arrowhead from the wood. He smiled at the man. "Yes." Still grinning, he returned to the shop. "Just long enough. I'll take them."

The passerby had retrieved his chicken and was now following John, waving it around for emphasis. "You can't loose a bow in the middle of town!"

The merchant gestured at the warhorse outside. "Glen, that's his mount."

"It was a gift," John snapped, "Bodkins, please."

The second man gasped. "You're giving him bodkins? Anti-armor arrows? Where did a guy like him get that horse?"

The merchant was now smiling too wide, trying to appear friendly and nonthreatening while choking back his panic. "Glen, shut the fuck up, please."

John pulled the bow again, experimentally. "I said it was a gift. A woman gave it to me right before she died. Now the man who killed her wants to kill me too."

He saw them exchange none-of-our-business glances. With a clunk, the merchant put a sheaf of arrows on the counter, bodkins and broadheads gleaming. "Anything else you want?"

"A few coins, I guess."

"A few," the merchant repeated. They both knew the bottle held a small fortune's worth of oil.

"Well, whatever you think is fair."

"I don't think I have enough coins for it to be fair."

"I guess I'll take what you have and a leather cloak, then. And some spare clothes."

Trey glared at the man sweating and groveling before him. "You failed."

Joseph stammered, "Well, I wouldn't say failed. I mean there were extenuating circumstances, and ..."

Trey held up his hand, but Joseph continued talking. "I really did all I could. I mean I didn't expect there to be weird spellwork on the ..."

"Shut up."

"Yes, sir."

Trey rubbed his forehead. "I am going to give you another chance. My agents tracked down where John lives."

"Really? I have been looking for that boy forever and I couldn't find heads nor tails of him. I honestly thought he was dead, you know?"

"Obviously you didn't look very hard because we asked your neighbor and she told us she received a letter from him a few years ago."

Joseph cleared his throat. "Well, I had heard rumors, of course. If they were true, and he was living in the middle of nowhere, I didn't really have the time to go check. My business has been busy ..."

Trey banged his fist on the table. "You didn't think to mention those rumors to me? That would have been nice to know earlier."

"Well, I didn't want to waste your time."

"I am going to send you to where he is supposedly living. I want you to convince him to come with me, however you can. Bring him to me, dead if you have to. Do you understand?" His glare made Joseph cower.

"Like I said, I am busy with my work...."

"Your company is on the verge of bankruptcy. If you want my money, you will do what I say. Understand?"

Joseph withered under Trey's gaze. "Right."

"Go. Wait outside."

Joseph gave a small bow and hurried out. As soon as he was out of eyesight, Trey sighed, turning to the soldier standing to one side. "That man is insufferable. Go with him, make sure he doesn't fuck up. If he can't convince the hunter, bring me his body."

"Joseph's or the hunter's body, sir?"

"Good question. Make it both. And bring me that stone."

John stared at an unhelpful road sign, scratching his beard, when a feeling came over him—the smell of old books. He pulled the gatestone from beneath his shirt. "Al-Haytham?"

"Greetings, John! How goes it?"

"Good, I suppose."

"Don't worry, I won't ask where you are."

"Well, I don't know where I am right now, so don't worry about it." John felt rather than heard the laughter on the other side.

"I just thought I would update you on the political situation in House Husniye."

John hesitated, gripping Horse's mane. "Go ahead."

"John, so you know, not letting your emotions leak through a gatestone connection is an important skill. Many a bureaucrat has lost a job because of it."

"I'll try to keep that in mind when I'm talking to a representative of the people who tried to kill me."

There was an awkward pause before al-Haytham replied. "My apologies. I should not have said that."

"It's fine. What's going on?"

"The short answer would simply be chaos. The long answer is, well, longer. Cecil is off trying to hunt down Ece. Trey is making moves. At this point, I and many others in Husniye's leadership, believe that if Olumtahss was in play we would not be able to support our claim to it."

"In other words, if I die," John said morosely.

"I was trying not to be morbid," said al-Haytham, apologetic.

"Cecil already mentioned that to me."

"Ah. Well, the good news is, it's now in House Husniye's best interest to keep you alive."

John didn't try to hide his bitterness. "So I should just head back then?"

"Oh no," al-Haytham said with a gasp. "That would be a terrible idea. I believe lobotomization was brought up. Until they break Husniye's spell and can hand it off to whomever they choose, they need a loyal, stupid gatekeeper, not an intelligent, independent thinker."

"Won't the Spire get the stone if I don't set an heir?"

"Oh yes. There is a time limit. Thus everyone is racing to get a hold of the stone."

"So … what do I do?" John flung his hands, palms up, in the air.

"If you want my sincere advice, I suggest you stay in hiding. Keep moving. You are a woodsman, so I am sure you can disappear."

John's breath hitched. "Wouldn't that ruin House Husniye?"

"I believe that House Husniye is already doomed."

John briefly sensed the sorrow seeping through the connection. "I'm sorry."

The emotion vanished as al-Haytham regained control. "It's not your fault. Husniye played a dangerous game, and it eventually caught up to her. It's likely that what's left of House Husniye will become nothing more than a vassal for another house."

"That's unfortunate." John rubbed his fingers over his smooth knife sheath.

"Even if you returned now, I doubt we could avoid it."

"Thanks for being honest."

"Of course. I owe you that, at least. You were dragged into this mess and deserve a way out of it. Once enough time has passed, seek out the Spire. If you hand over Olumtahss without question, you may get out of this unscathed."

"Haytham …"

"Good luck, John. If anything changes, I'll let you know."

〜

Trey stared intently at the warlock. "I want him dead."

The other man immediately burst into raucous laughter. "I love that about you, Max! So blunt, so eager. No whispers in dark alleys, just demanding what you want. Now, who did you want dead? Romanov?"

"No, the hunter, fool."

"Ahh, John the Mighty Hunter, killer of nightmares and survivor extraordinaire! It's shocking he's still alive, isn't it?"

Trey sank into a comfortable chair, grumbling. "Quit the drama." A servant stole forward to fill his raised teacup.

"Don't you already have agents dealing with it?" The warlock smirked as the servant slipped from the room.

"I like to hedge my bets."

"Fine. I have something that should be perfect for the job. A failed experiment."

"Failed?" Trey raised an eyebrow, "What was the experiment?"

"I've been trying to see if it's possible to move someone a great distance without a gatestone!" Impossibly, the warlock's smile grew wider. "As it turns out, it's entirely possible. Unfortunately, there are some, uh, side effects. More experiments will be necessary."

"You want to send an assassin?"

"Well, there is this hunter that my wonderful patron wants dead, so I figured—haha—kill two birds with one stone!"

Trey stared down the man before laughing himself. "Funny man. Unfortunately, we don't know where the hunter is. The gatestone is stopping us from scrying."

The warlock stood, animated. "That's the beauty of it. Scrying is like searching through a telescope. Easy to miss things. However, if you see from above...."

"I don't follow."

"How does teleportation work? One second a person is here, the next over there!" The warlock was gesturing wildly now. "They do not zip through the air like a bird, or else there would be far more holes in walls." He laughed at his own joke. "No, they go between."

"You want to launch someone into the aether."

"Not just that. He will be in a ship of sorts, sailing the between. Imagine if you could travel to a gatestone from anywhere! It would revolutionize things. No more dealing with two fixed gates. I shiver just thinking about it! And from the aether, certain things are easier to spot. Like the openings a gatestone makes in the aether!"

Trey tilted his head to the side. "I guess the reason nobody uses this method is that having someone floating around in the aether is not healthy."

"Like I said, many side effects," the warlock said with a crafty grin. "Do you want to watch?"

"No!"

"Liar."

Trey laughed again, then nodded. "All right, let's see."

A few minutes later, the two men stood in front of a cell. Iron bars separated them from a bedraggled man with long, greasy hair and ragged clothes. He pounded the wall with his fists, leaving smears of blood on the stone. The warlock gestured to the man. "The biggest problem is exposure to raw magic …"

Trey interrupted, deadpan. "It turns you into a monster."

"Oh please, take all the fun out of this, why don't you?"

"Bit of a fighter this one," Trey remarked.

"Oh, yes indeed."

"It's the fellow that spat on my shoes earlier this year, isn't it?"

"Good memory! Now, the plan. I send this poor fool to where he needs to go. Through a wild gate."

"I have heard that term before. Shamans of old would use them to travel?"

The warlock nodded eagerly. "It turns out that gates are relatively easy to make."

"Sure, if you want to grow extra arms."

"Please, growing new arms is a very rare mutation, at least with raw magic. Of course, if you are looking for more arms, it's possible to manipulate things to make that a little more likely."

"Uh-huh." Trey's eyes widened at the possibilities.

"But yes, it's possible to do it safely, if you are skilled. But keeping someone other than a mage safe in the aether is very difficult and dangerous, practically impossible to do remotely."

"So, you'll drop him directly on our hunter, then?"

Bobbing his head, the warlock said, "Unfortunately, I cannot be that exact. Just the general area. However, the shining magic of Olumtahss should draw any Twisted toward it, especially if I tweak its behavior. Anyway, let's take this subject to the test chambers, and I can begin!"

Trey nodded at two soldiers, who stepped forward and unlocked the door.

# 14

Cecil leaned around a corner to spot two white-masked guards standing at attention before a building entrance. The complex was surrounded by a wall, complete with patrolling guards on top. This was one of three entrances, and the only one that seemed to be accessible to the public. Somewhere inside was either information or Yeela herself, and Cecil needed in.

A polite cough behind him broke his concentration. A local militia officer, club dangling from his waist, greeted him. Cecil looked him up and down, noting his only armor was a metal cap and some vambraces. "Can I help you?"

"Well, sir, I have received several reports that someone set off an explosion in the middle of the street, and you seem to match the description. Would you mind coming with me?"

Cecil tugged a pouch of coins from his belt. "I'm busy. Take this, go away. Unless you want to deal with one of House Husniye's top enforcers."

The bag landed at the militiaman's feet with a jingle. He eyed Cecil, hand resting on his sword hilt, then the coins. He picked up the coins, gave a small nod, then power-walked away. Cecil smirked and turned back to the White Masks complex.

The fact that the White Masks seemed to operate outside the local laws said a lot about their political pull on the island. If they were involved in Ece's kidnapping, the whole thing just became far more complicated. As he watched, a couple strode past the two guards, who ignored them. There was likely some form of magical security, and maybe more checkpoints inside.

Cecil turned around, annoyed, at another polite cough behind him. This time, his companions included several better-armored men. "Didn't I bribe you?" he asked the militiaman.

The man stepped forward. "We thank you for your very generous donation to the Hydra Island Defense Fund. However, we must ask you to leave the island."

"You're a lot braver now that you have your friends with you."

"Well, yeah. Of course. That's usually how it works."

Cecil sighed. "Well. I have something I need to do before I leave."

"You set off an explosion. In the street."

"I am looking for—"

"Yes, we know, you've told many people why you're here. But you need to leave. Work through your grief in a nondestructive way, please. Now please, follow me and— Hey!"

Cecil had taken off in a dead sprint toward the White Masks complex. At the entrance, he stopped, resting his hands on his knees, huffing. The two White Masks stood stoic, seeming not to notice him. Across the square, stood more military men, some looking amused.

"Do you want a mask?"

Cecil jumped at a nearby voice. A dog peered at him from a window in the wall. A concierge booth. Not a dog, but a person in a brown dog mask.

"Can I just enter? I have business inside."

"Put on your mask before you continue." The dog's face had no obvious breathing holes, yet the voice was not muffled.

"I don't have one." He tugged at the door next to the concierge's window, but it would not budge.

"You need to be wearing a mask."

Cecil stifled a groan. "My apologies. I'll take a mask then." A gloved hand gestured to a sign on the wall, where a drawing of a coin next to a mask was barely illuminated by mage light. Cecil dropped a coin into the hand, the dog mask turned away briefly, then offered him a simple wood mask, with crude holes for the eyes and mouth. Cecil grimaced. "Don't you have a nicer one?"

Dog Mask held up two fingers, and Cecil sighed, producing another coin. This time, the concierge came back holding a red mask with horns and a deranged smile. Cecil gave the clerk a dirty look and donned the mask. With a click, the door unlocked.

Behind the walls, a market stretched before him. He strode the major thoroughfare, sun streaming through the colorful cloth overhead. He passed a cage full of men, many of prime age. A masked customer haggled with a merchant in a blue mask, trying to get one of the scrawnier ones thrown in for free. The next cage held a mix of ragged and skinny men and women.

He paused for a moment in front of a cage holding a single child. He couldn't tell the exact age, but the child hadn't reached puberty. A merchant in a mask painted to resemble a turquoise dolphin stepped up. "Are you interested?"

Cecil stared a moment, then walked past silently, grateful that his mask hid his expression. He wandered aimlessly for a while. The keep, a large stone building, guarded by two more White Masks, dominated the small market. He noted that none of the merchants in the open market wore white masks and their slaves all appeared to be ordinary men and women. He made his way to the keep.

As he approached, he noted the masks of the guards had a single diagonal line crossing them. One extended a hand as Cecil ascended. "What are you seeking?"

Cecil tried to keep the bitterness out of his voice. "I heard you obtained one of my favorite prostitutes. I thought I would treat myself."

Above the doorway, a stone suddenly glowed. The guard shook his head "That was a lie."

Cecil fidgeted, then blurted, "I'm looking to buy." No light this time, and the man gestured for him to pass through. He glanced around. The inside of the building was well lit, and all the merchants wore white masks. Every woman on display was beautiful, dressed elegantly, and done up with makeup. All the men also wore sharp clothing, many with swords belted to their waists. There were no cages or chains. None were needed. Each wore black collars around their throats, marked with a symbol in white.

Cecil stopped in front of an information booth, crewed by another masked woman. She glanced up from the book she was reading. "May I help you?"

"I am looking for someone specific. Name: Yeela."

"A seller named Yeela?"

Cecil shook his head. "No, a slave."

"Then you are looking for something formerly named Yeela, correct?"

Cecil stared before mumbling, "Yes, I suppose."

"Wait here." She disappeared through a side door. Cecil waited awkwardly, trying not to look at the merchandise. After some time, the woman came back.

"Someone will be here to help you shortly."

Cecil sighed and leaned against the counter, sword gently thumping the wood. After a while, a voice startled him.

"Around here, people consider asking for a slave by name a faux pas. If you are trying to recover a relative, we have proper channels to do that."

Cecil studied the man. Like every other white mask, he wore all black, with no skin showing. However, unlike the others Cecil had seen, this mask was featureless. He'd heard you could tell which subgroup the slavers were part of based on the mask they wore. Cecil could never figure it out, but he had never heard of a blank mask. There were supposed to be rules. "I'm sorry. She was my favorite prostitute. I thought I would treat myself."

The masked man leaned in closer. "Well, she has already been ... processed. Of course, that means the price is high"

Cecil clenched his jaw, and muttered, "That's fine. Take me to her."

A few moments later, Cecil stood before a woman in a red-trimmed dress who knelt on the ground. "Hello, Yeela." Cecil heard sorrow in his voice.

She stared into the distance. "Hello, sir." She wore makeup, hair cascaded down her back, and lace framed her cleavage. A black collar circled her neck.

The blank-faced man asked, "Would you like to try her?"

"I've … already tried her a number of times." The man chuckled as Cecil turned to face him, grateful for the mask. "How much to buy?"

"Three coffers."

"Three? Sir, that is far too much!"

"Fully broken in, she will do whatever you want. Nothing left up here." The man tapped the top of her head. "Anything you want." He stressed the word anything, drawing it out like a long kiss.

Three coffers was expensive even for a fully collared slave. Expensive, period. A ridiculous sum. "I'll give you a bag."

"A bag! You insult me!" The man stomped his foot. The mask made it hard to tell what he thought, and all his body language was stiff and jerky.

"I don't have more than a bag on me. Do you take credit?"

"Depends on the credit." The masked man leaned in close. "If you are backed by a viable house that can guarantee payment, then yes. For example, if you were from House Husniye, we would take credit from them. For now, at least."

"Fuck you."

"Three coffers."

"You were already paid for this, weren't you?"

"Excuse me?"

"To help Trey. You already got paid by Trey to help arrange this whole thing. You probably kidnapped Ece as well. Used Yeela to lure her in."

"Oh my, you do take all the fun out of this whole cloak and dagger business, don't you?" The man leaned back, amused. "But you know the dance. I won't admit to anything."

Cecil's muscles tensed as the masked man wagged a finger at him. "If you try anything, anything at all, you won't make it out of here alive." Cecil took a deep breath, realizing that his hand had moved over to his sword. "Many of our slaves know how to fight. They make excellent bodyguards, always loyal. Never wavering. Very popular. Have you ever considered getting one?"

"I am not paying three coffers. You know that's ridiculous."

"I think you will pay. You seem desperate."

Cecil paused, thinking. "Well. I would guess Trey wanted to make sure there were no more loose ends. He can be very thorough. He probably wanted her dead, not enslaved."

"And yet there she is. Alive and well. You may even be able to get some information out of her. Some of her memories are still there. Nobody wants a slave that forgot how to walk. Three coffers."

"If Trey finds out, he will be furious."

The masked man leaned in close. "Why do you think I am asking for so much?"

Cecil arrived back at House Husniye's gatestone, with Yeela in tow, without incident. They managed to dodge the Hydra Island militia thanks to a small port attached to the slave market. Cecil contacted al-Haytham to clear the room before he and Yeela arrived, and he was waiting for them when they came through. "Were you followed?"

Cecil shook his head. "I was careful. But it is only a matter of time before word gets back to Trey."

Ahu entered the room carrying cups of ginger tea, a traditional means of settling the stomach after a gatestone trip. She stopped in her tracks when she spotted Yeela. "You brought a collared back? Are you crazy?"

Cecil gestured wearily. "This is what's left of Ece's lover. She's officially licensed by the White Masks, so she doesn't have any hidden commands. We need to try and extract some memories from her."

Al-Haytham produced some spellstones from one of his many pockets and peered at Yeela while Cecil sipped his tea.

Al-Haytham stroked his beard thoughtfully. "I don't have enough expertise in mind manipulation. We could go to an expert, but it would be expensive and would not guarantee any results."

"This is the only lead I have right now." Cecil finished the tea, handing the cup back to Ahu. "Speaking of expense, I had to buy Yeela. I talked him down from three coffers to two...." Cecil trailed off, and al-Haytham winced while Ahu's jaw dropped.

Yeela spoke, startling all of them. "Is there anything I can do to help, Master?"

Cecil snapped. "I wasn't talking to you."

"I am sorry, Master."

The room lapsed into awkward silence. At last, Cecil turned to Yeela. "I'm sorry. Listen, we are going to try and undo what was done to you. You won't be able to live like you did before, but you can at least get … something back. And maybe answer my questions."

Yeela did not respond.

Al-Haytham peered at Cecil, frowning. "The chances of this yielding anything helpful is slim."

"I had to try." Cecil stared at Yeela.

Al-Haytham continued, slipping into lecture mode, much to Cecil's chagrin. "Memories erased cannot be recovered. You cannot unshatter a pot. All we can hope for is they missed enough to make it worthwhile. And as well, just because she is officially licensed by the White Masks doesn't mean she can't have hidden commands implanted. Only their reputation stops them from doing that, and they have in the past. Furthermore—" al-Haytham was cut off when a pale-yellow light filled the room. The collar around Yeela's throat glowed brightly, and a crackling sound, like the sound of dry leaves being crushed filled the room.

"What?" Cecil exclaimed. Before anyone could move, the collar fell from her neck. Yeela moved quickly, jumping forward and tackling Cecil to the floor. She reached for his belt and pulled the dagger free.

With a laugh, he grabbed her wrist and twisted her arm hard, freeing the dagger from her grasp. Grinning from ear to ear, Cecil said, "Ece taught you a few tricks! I'm Cecil. She might have mentioned me."

189

Immediately, Yeela stopped struggling and stared wide-eyed at Cecil. She was quiet as Ahu placed a blanket around her and a cup of tea in her hand, only murmuring, "Thank you."

As al-Haytham inspected the collar with a magnifying glass, Cecil sat across from her, waiting. She took a few sips of her tea, staring into space. Cecil waited for her to make eye contact before speaking.

"So, you and Ece were ..."

Bitterly, Yeela snapped, "We fucked, yeah."

Cecil said, "I was going to say lovers. You had a fight?" The glare she directed at Cecil would melt snow. He returned her gaze with a sly smile. "Was it about money?"

"Fuck you. You know what it was about? Me being trapped on that whore island with no way out. You think I wanted to run a whorehouse for the rest of my life?" She continued as the blanket fell from her shoulders. "Then along came Ece. She was ... she was nice to me. I am grateful. I really am. But she refused to ..." Yeela stabbed a finger in his direction. "I wanted to leave! But she insisted I stay in that fucking shithole! Told me to 'be patient.'"

"She was trying to protect you."

"Don't you start with that bullshit too!"

"Bullshit? Look what happened."

"Do you think this would have happened if I had been at House Husniye, huh? She was embarrassed by me."

Cecil looked to al-Haytham for help, but al-Haytham was too engrossed in studying the broken collar.

Yeela spat, "So where is she? Hiding from me?"

Quietly, Cecil said, "She's missing."

Yeela recoiled, genuine shock on her face.

Cecil continued, "We think Trey got her. All her contracts are still intact, so she's alive. We just don't know where she is."

Yeela dropped into her chair, and Ahu gently placed the blanket around her, patting her on the shoulder and saying, "Husniye is dead, in case you hadn't heard."

"I hadn't. How?"

Cecil hesitated before responding. "Ambushed. Trey again, we believe, with some help from the Spire. Ece went missing at the same time. And the gatestone, you know, Olumtahss is ... Husniye managed to make a contract with a new heir before she died. A man named John the Hunter. A random hermit. He's missing too. It's all gone to shit. I have been trying to track down Ece, so John can abdicate the stone to her, but her trail went cold." He lapsed into silence as Yeela continued to sip her tea, looking drained.

Eventually, al-Haytham spoke. "How did you break free?"

"Ece was worried, so she gave me a spellstone to protect my mind."

Al-Haytham furrowed his eyebrows. "You managed to keep it hidden?"

"I swallowed it before they noticed."

Al-Haytham produced a notebook from one of his pockets. "When did you swallow the spellstone?"

"They put me in a carriage and locked it. I managed to wiggle out of the ropes and swallow it."

Al-Haytham nodded, making a note. "Where is it now?"

Yeela pointed at her stomach.

"How did you keep it from discharging ... Never mind. Let's not ask that. How did they lure Ece in?"

"We had a meeting we had already arranged. I told them everything. I was like a puppet, I couldn't control my own body, I just ..." Yeela trailed off, eyes watery.

"I'm sorry, but a few more questions. Do you have any idea where they could have brought Ece?"

Yeela gave a tiny, pained chuckle. "Ece put some other spells on the spellstone. Including a way to find her."

Cecil, Ahu, and al-Haytham all leaned forward, eager. Al-Haytham spoke first. "Can it tell us exactly where she is?"

"Location and distance."

Al-Haytham clapped his hands together. "Wonderful!" Cecil leaned back with a sigh of relief.

Ahu rubbed Yeela on the shoulder. "Are you okay?"

"No, I am not." Yeela wiped tears away.

Ahu put an arm around her. "You want to talk about it?"

"I remember what they did to me."

Cecil looked uncomfortable. "I'm sorry you got pulled into this mess."

Yeela snapped, "If only I had been in a protected place like House Husniye."

Cecil grimaced. "I don't think bringing a prostitute here would have gone over well."

Flatly, Yeela replied, "She never hired me."

Cecil blinked. "What?"

"She never paid me anything."

Cecil looked away, embarrassed. "Oh. So you two really had a whole ... thing going then."

She said nothing for a moment, then blurted, "I'm not broken."

Ahu rubbed her shoulder again. "We know, dear. Just let us take care of you for a bit."

Cecil watched them leave, then turned to al-Haytham. "Ece is terrible at relationships."

"Always has been."

# 15

John eyed the farm as he strode by, Horse following. Dismounting did not make him any less conspicuous, but his butt was sore, and he wanted to stretch his legs. Sticking to well-maintained roads was unwise, but traveling through the forest had led to an unfortunate incident with a low branch. With the midday sun beating down, the field workers had taken refuge in the shade. John hoped they didn't notice him.

He'd made slow progress sticking to the backroads, but he was nearing the village. Now there were no more side trails. Everyone living here relied on one main road, which they called the Old Stone Road, and it ended near the edge of the forest, close to John's cabin. There was no avoiding it.

John patted the horse. "I guess I could leave you here, huh? More incognito? But there's still a way to go. Once we get into the forest beyond my cabin, we can hide. They won't find us there." John mounted again.

With a snort, Horse picked up speed until he and John were flying down the ancient, well-built road at full gallop. The ground beneath his feet was a blur, and his eyes watered in the wind. John laughed as they thundered on, over hills and valleys, past the old watchtowers that had been repurposed as farmhouses, past toppled obelisks now covered in vines, ignoring everyone they passed.

As the sun moved across the sky, John recognized the landscape. Late in the afternoon, they reached Anderson's village. The closest civilization to his own home. He dismounted close to a tree, and leaving Horse to graze, made his way into town. Despite Obi's gifts, he still needed to resupply.

He sauntered in, surprised and grateful to see the streets empty. He made his way to Anderson's door and knocked.

Nothing. That was odd. He knocked again and called out. "Anderson? It's me."

Now John heard quick footsteps. The door opened a crack, and Anderson's face appeared, eyes wide. "John!" he whispered. "Run!" Then he grunted, and a sword emerged point-first from his chest.

John stumbled backward, shouting "Fuck!" As the door flew open, Anderson flopped forward onto the ground. Somewhere behind him, John heard Horse scream.

A man appeared in the doorway, flicking his sword to the side to remove the blood. Between them, Anderson lay quivering and gasping for air. For a moment, John froze, staring in shock. Then the man stepped forward. His sword thumped against the door frame.

John launched himself at the intruder. The man tried to bring his sword forward but it had caught on the doorframe, delaying the swing for the split second John needed. John slammed his foot into the man's knee. It sounded like a stick breaking, and the man fell hard to one side, his shoulder slamming the ground. Somehow, he held onto the sword and swung it wildly, but John dodged it easily as he unsheathed his knife. He swept his dagger across the man's neck, then watched his eyes bulge as the life force drained from his body. The man died, fury painted on his face.

A small stain spread across John's shirt. The sword must have nicked him. Before he could look closer, a cough caught his attention. Anderson was still breathing.

He scrambled across the ground to his friend, cradling his head and shoulders in his arms. "Anderson!"

"Don't … blame yourself," Anderson wheezed, blood staining his teeth.

"Tell me what to do. I can … Just tell me what to do." John looked at his friend's torso. Blood pumped from the wound.

"Don't …" Anderson began and gasped again. "B …blame …"

John's tears flowed freely now. "No no no no! Don't."

"Your … self …" Anderson finished, then was still.

He was still looking down at his friend when he heard footsteps behind him.

"They didn't listen to my orders."

He wiped the tears that had fallen on Anderson's face, and stood up, turning to face whoever was behind him.

His uncle stammered, backing away. "I … I … I'm sorry about your friend there. I told the soldiers to hold back!" Horse's front hooves and chest were splashed with blood, and two men lay dead at the animal's feet.

His uncle smiled, his tone suddenly soothing and soft. "Now John, I was just trying to take you home, that's all. These soldiers, they just love killing. It happens, all right?"

His uncle stepped forward, one hand extended toward John. "Really, I'm so, so sorry for your loss."

John caught the knife that was halfway to his chest, gripping his uncle's wrist hard and twisting. The man's weapon fell to the ground with a thud.

"Uh," his uncle gasped.

Before he could continue, John's fist connected with his face with a meaty thump. As the man's knees buckled, John shifted his grip to hold him up. Blood poured from his uncle's nose. John hit him again. And again. And again. When John finally let go, his uncle hit the ground with a thump.

John glanced at his own bloody knuckles for a moment before taking a slow, smooth breath. He glanced at his uncle, whimpering at his feet. Then he checked Anderson, who lay unmoving by the door. A primal, furious scream came out of his mouth and he brought his foot up, then down on his uncle's skull. And again. And again. And again. There was a crunching sound. John turned and limped back to Horse, leaving behind bloody footsteps.

⌒

John slumped on Horse's back as they entered the forest. The sun was setting on the path before them. Horse nickered, and John's head snapped up. Ahead, he spotted the silhouette of a man, standing still. He wore a cloak with its hood pulled over his face. John attempted a casual wave. Horse stepped to the side, trying to put as much space as possible between them and the figure on the narrow path. Now the man took a few halting steps toward them, limping.

"Hey," John greeted him. "Bum leg, huh?"

The man said nothing but shuffled closer.

John's heart beat faster. He patted Horse's neck nervously, and Horse took a few backward steps, trying to put more distance between them. "Can you speak?" John heard his own voice shaking.

John saw the figure's proportions weren't quite human. He clutched at the straps that held the bow to his back. He loosed it just as the creature lunged at him.

Horse reared, striking the creature in the shoulder. John yelped, fell from Horse, and slammed into the ground, clutching his bow to his chest. He lay still for a second, gasping, trying to get his lungs working again. He looked up at the figure.

The thing's hood had been knocked back, revealing a human face, green eyes, tanned skin, and a well-trimmed beard. One side of the face was offset a hand's width from the other side. Eyes fixed on John, it flashed a toothy, deranged grin.

Arrow finally in hand, John yelled, "Twisted!" He loosed an arrow and it hissed into the thing's chest. It screamed, clutching at the arrow, then crouched. The being paused a moment, then jumped, higher than humanly possible. John dove to the side and the thing landed where he had been with a crunch, leg bones shattering. It howled into the sky as John scrambled away, pulling out another arrow. Blood pooled beneath the shards of bone emerging from its skin. John's arrow grazed its temple, stripping skin to reveal a streak of red and white. One of its eyes glared at John as the other rolled in its socket.

The creature skittered across the ground on all fours like a spider as John dodged again. He missed his footing and slid, rolling back to his feet. His left arm stung where the broadhead tip of the arrow had nicked it. The Twisted slammed a fist into the ground, then screamed in pain as its arm fractured. Then it grinned at him with sharp teeth. John put another arrow in its chest just as it lunged.

This time, its legs buckled and it sat, gasping for air. John nocked another arrow, hoping to finish the Twisted off at last. Then, it vibrated. The bone shards sticking from its flesh lengthened.

John pawed at his throat, bile rising at the noise.

Suddenly, it stood, the gnarled bone spurs forming two massive feet. It began to walk, crackling with each step.

John's hand shook. "Steady. Steady. Steady," he whispered to himself. He pulled the bow back and put an arrow into the thing's eye. It screamed, clutching at its face. "Horse! Go for the head."

Horse charged forward, rearing. With the full weight of his body behind the move, he drove his front hooves into the Twisted's skull. The screaming stopped, and it lay still.

John sat down, hard. "I hate Twisted."

Horse stepped over and nudged him. John patted him on the nose. He spotted a gash on his arm. "When did that happen?" He made his way to the brook running parallel to the path and slid down the embankment. Horse made his way more carefully and clopped into the stream.

"Come here," John beckoned, and when Horse splashed close, he scooped water in his hands and released it over his bloody flanks. As John tended to Horses's

wounds, he muttered, "I'm so sorry. This is my fault."
Horse headbutted him tenderly.

Next, John saw to his own wounds—the gash in his
chest from the fight with the soldier along with the spot
where the arrow grazed his arm. Staggering from dizziness,
he pulled himself back up the embankment with the help
of a tree root and collapsed at the edge of the path. He
stared at the tangled mass of blood and flesh that had been
the Twisted before rising to roll it over with a grunt.

He removed his dagger from its sheath and reclaimed
his arrowheads from the corpse. He paused as he noticed
an insignia on the tattered clothing. Two towers on a hill.
House DuFort.

John swallowed, then lifted Olumtahss and stared at it.
"Never asked how it stops me from being tracked." He
considered that if House DuFort knew the general area to
look for him—and from the incident in the village, they
did—they could flood it with Twisted to flush him out.
He looked over at Horse. "Time to go."

Horse trotted off as soon as he mounted, moving at a
faster pace than before. At last, they stopped in a clearing.
He slipped from Horse's back and collapsed to the ground,
more exhausted than ever. He recognized the spot. He'd
often hunted rabbits here, but now the memory seemed
like someone else's life.

John stood up after a while, wiping his tears away.
Darkness had fallen. Horse stood patiently nearby. He
moved to strip off the saddle. "I am so sorry." He noticed
blood on the leather from Horse's wounded flank. "Should
we keep going? Keep riding?" He let the saddle fall into a
patch of grass and sat beside it. His eyelids drooped. "I

dunno," he answered himself. He lay back against the saddle and fell asleep.

⌒

"John?"

John gasped and bolted upright. The moon cast a pale light on everything. He glanced around but didn't see anyone.

"Sorry, did I wake you up?" Cecil's voice continued.

John lifted the gatestone on its chain. "Yeah, but it's fine."

"I am back at House Husniye. We got a lucky break. We know where Ece is."

John stared up at the sky, the stars familiar and comforting. "Ah."

"I thought you would be more excited."

"Tough day. How soon can you get her?"

"Well, that's the problem. We are pretty sure she is being held in a fortress."

"Can you take the fortress in the time that's left?"

"Probably not." Cecil sighed. "But we are going to try, and …"

"Cecil," John interrupted, "al-Haytham told me it's important not to let your emotions leak through during stone-to-stone communication. You're doing a terrible job."

"It's … I'll admit the situation appears hopeless. But we have to try."

John mused. "At this point, I am just going to hide. I figure eventually the Spire will show up. I'm sorry, but I don't know how to help. I mean, once the month is up, won't Trey just kill Ece? Why keep her alive?"

"Well, the Spire would be rather upset. She's still a gatekeeper."

"She already has a gatestone? You don't have to stay close to keep it from degrading?"

John heard the pride in Cecil's voice. "No. Being present helps, but just having a gatekeeper is enough to keep them going. Most gatestones have multiple gatekeepers who take shifts, but Ece handles it alone, remotely."

"Hmm. If it was damaged, could she repair it remotely?"

"Ha, she's not that good."

"If it was damaged, Ece would need to be present to fix it, right?"

"Right."

John thought for a moment. "If you were to damage her gatestone, Trey would have to bring her, right?"

Cecil sounded a little panicked. "Oh, no. No, no."

"So Trey wouldn't have to—"

"Purposefully damaging a gatestone would … The Spire would be very upset. Very upset. If a house did that on purpose, the Spire would probably end the house. So it's not an option. Plus, it's a very important gatestone in Wetstone."

"Not an option for House Husniye."

"Look, just stay hidden. As long as Trey doesn't find you, it will be over for you one way or another. Either we get Ece first and bring her to you, or the Spire grabs you.

They'll probably let you go in exchange for your cooperation."

"Probably," John blurted. "A Twisted tried to kill me."

"What? Glad you are alive."

"It wore DuFort colors."

"That has implications. I wouldn't put anything past Trey. I'll stay in touch. Just ... try to stay alive. And don't do anything stupid."

# 16

John stared up at the night sky, grass rustling beneath him whenever he shifted. Thoughts flooded his mind. He considered his dirt-encrusted hands. The soil here had small amounts of natural nullstone. He remembered Zen explaining that's why the Twisted avoided this place. "It's like a magical desert—a holy place. Not enough Storm for them to survive, so they don't like to congregate." The spot was also too rocky and infertile for farming. Thanks to the nullstone, fertility spells wouldn't hold. Poor in magic, poor in soil.

Nullstone could be worth plenty to the right buyer, but its very nature made it difficult to locate. The landscape was dotted with old mines as prospectors had tried sifting the region. But the only deposits large enough to be useful were scattered in the mountains in seams the size of a pinky finger. Getting there was so difficult, most quit in disappointment. For that reason, the stone road had been abandoned years ago when it reached the base of the mountains. Even those who managed to get to the mountains had no certainty of finding anything of value. The region held no strategic value, no natural resources, no Storm, and little food—making it the perfect place for John to avoid and evade detection.

"Why was Husniye here?" John spoke into the darkness. Obi had told him she would have had to shift for herself the equivalent of a few days' travel to make it to his doorstep. Was that a few days on foot or by horseback? He had no obvious answers.

He held the gatestone up to the stars. Their light swirled like sparkles on a river. Closing his eyes, John laid back and concentrated. He felt the gatestone in his hand, the earth against his back. He furrowed his brows and felt a sensation like floating in a boat in a vast ocean, rocking gently back and forth. Suddenly came a smell of old books, and he reached out with his mind.

"Yes, what is it?" Al-Haytham's sleepy voice broke the silence. John froze, the hand with the gatestone still outstretched toward the stars.

"Al-Haytham? Um … I think I just called you?"

"You did."

"Sorry, I didn't mean to. Well, I sort of did, but not you."

"What?"

"I was looking for answers. Go back to sleep."

"I doubt I will be able to do that. I thought there was yet another emergency. With all the chaos, I have taken to sleeping with a communication stone. Now I am quite awake."

"I am sorry," John insisted. "I was just wondering why Husniye would travel to a Storm-barren land." Recognizing the faux pas, he added, "Magically barren, I mean."

"I wasn't aware she did."

205

"That's ... where my house is. The nearest village is on the edge of the barren lands. We brought her body there in a cart."

"That makes sense. It's probably the only reason Li was able to reach you." Al-Haytham paused. "Wait. Husniye was attacked by Summons?"

"Twisted. Yeah."

"On barren land? Well, that is curious. It would take quite a powerful mage to do that. Give me a moment."

John heard sheets rustling and protested, "No, you don't have to get out of bed."

"I may as well. You've piqued my interest."

John listened as small noises drifted through the stone. His attention was wandering when al-Haytham's voice jolted him.

"I assumed she was injured and fled toward the barren land, not the other way around. I have a map here. Where is the house?"

"End of the Old Stone Road."

"Ah, yes. Built by ... well, the name escapes me, but they were hoping to colonize the area. Ran into trouble when they could no longer rely on magic. Interesting. I was wondering how a hunter so unaffiliated stayed alive. Some others speculated you were some sort of hero or warrior in hiding."

"Really? I wish. Maybe then I could have saved ..." John started. "Sorry. I am letting my feelings leak through. You warned me about that."

Gently, al-Haytham asked, "What happened?"

John's eyes prickled. Hoarsely, he whispered, "They killed him. My friend. Anderson. He ... His last words were, 'Don't blame yourself.' His last words were trying to comfort me. What did I do to deserve that, you know? I was a ... I ran away from home. I lived in the woods like a savage. Just to get away from everything." John's voice broke. "And he was always there for me. He lent me books. Talked to me. Took care of me. Saved my life once, after a Twisted attack. Nursed me for weeks."

"Sounds like he was a good friend."

"I never checked inside the house. I didn't see if Elizabeth was okay. I ran." John wailed. "I should have checked. I should have known. I ... I could have sent a letter. I could have done something."

"If you could travel back in time, there might been something you could have done. But you don't. Things happen, John. The ant that was trodden looks up into the sky and bemoans his fate, asking why the gods would smite him so. But the gods were simply walking to the outhouse. What you're caught in is far beyond your ability to know or handle." Al-Haytham trailed off for a moment. "Treasure your memories of him. He sounds like a good man. If I had to give you one piece of advice, it would be the same. Don't blame yourself."

It took a while for John to stop crying.

Finally, John asked, "Are you still there?"

"Yes, I am," al-Haytham replied.

"Thanks. And sorry."

"Not a problem. You have been through a lot these last few days. Listen, this map? It has some notes in Husniye's writing. Apparently, there are some old ruins in the area. A house belonging to a researcher named ... Shielken? It looks like he was researching gates. That must have been her destination. I don't know how they found out that she was going there. Even I didn't know her plans. But that's probably where they ambushed her."

John wiped his eyes. "Where is this ruin?"

Top of the mountain in the barren zone."

"Ahh." John breathed.

"I am going to go to bed now, John. Ok?"

"Thank you. Really."

"Of course."

The connection ended.

John remained motionless, observing the stars. Finally, he fell asleep.

~

John woke to see Horse's face directly above his own. He reached up and patted the white muzzle, then sat up. "You know," he said, "I think I have seen those ruins, from a distance." As he struggled to his feet, he saw the state of Horse's wounds. "I'm really sorry," he said, touching Horse's side. With water and his shirt, he did his best to wash away the crusty blood, then placed a spare shirt under the saddle so the leather wouldn't rub the cuts.

"I think I want to go have a look. I am tired of being an ant. What do you say, Horse?"

In reply, Horse began to trot, and together they headed for the mountain.

The journey took some days. The trees grew more sparse and the ground more rocky, but Horse was sure-footed. On the first afternoon, they found a makeshift shelter John had made a few years back, in a clearing overgrown with grass and blue wildflowers. The next morning, a beautiful deer wandered into the clearing. John put an arrow through its heart. For the rest of the day, John concentrated on butchering and smoking the meat while Horse rested and feasted on grass. That night, they slept with full bellies, warm and comfortable in the shelter.

The next morning, he spotted a bank of worrisome clouds on the horizon. It was time to move on. He couldn't take all the smoked meat, and though he hated to leave provisions behind, at least he had enough for a few days, plus a hide to sell.

He cleaned Horse's wounds again. Then, as they made their way up the rocky terrain, John spotted something. He tugged Horse's mane to bring the stallion to a stop. John stared at the small plant poking out between two rocks. He laughed and scrambled from the saddle.

Anderson had once given John a drawing of a rare plant. "This is a powerful medicinal," he had explained. "Grows in the foothills. If you see any while you're on one of your hunting trips, will you bring it to me?" John had spent the next three months scouring the countryside for the plant before finding one. He'd brought it back to Anderson dried, the purple flower still vivid.

John had tried to insist it was no big deal, but Elizabeth had seen through him. She had insisted her husband give him something in payment. They had presented him with the knife he now wore at his hip. He used it to cut a shoot off the plant, placed it into his pouch, and continued on his way, sniffling just a little.

Finally, they reached a summit. Below, a valley rolled and another mountain loomed beyond it. In the distance, at the peak, he saw what they were looking for: a single square structure, one window visible, and what might be stone stairs leading up to the building. He noticed something else. Around the stone hut, the ground was scorched. In the valley, many of the trees had darkened trunks. "Well, there it is. The ruin Husniye was looking for," John said to Horse. He nudged the stallion's flank and they began their descent into the valley.

John stepped up the last step, huffing. Horse followed, making grumpy noises. The stone building lay straight ahead at the end of a flagstone path. The surrounding ground was swampy, wispy green grass clinging to the peat underneath. To the right, lay a crater that looked like someone had hurled a large boulder from a great height, dislodging a large circle of peat. A fire had ripped through the forest in the valley, leaving blackened trunks, but it had stopped at the edge of the bog.

The flagstones shifted slightly as he stepped across them. Most were partly sunken in the soggy earth, but he made it across without getting too wet. Horse tromped across the wet ground, his hooves making a slurping sound each time he pulled them out.

The house was built of local stone, using a naturally flat rocky outcropping on the plateau as the foundation. Large blocks, piled haphazardly, form the walls. John marveled at the effort someone had gone to to build the wall, yet how little regard they'd had for its appearance.

John paused in the doorway, surveying the structure. The stone floor, also local but a darker material, was covered in strange carvings. In one corner were the remnants of a bookcase, in another, the rotten remains of furniture.

As for the ceiling, John stared at it, frowning. It looked like a single block, a lid dropped on a pot. This made little sense because stone wasn't strong horizontally and normally required arches to act as a roof.

Maybe the room was small enough that it didn't matter. Each side could accommodate only four men of his height lying end to end. He looked again at the carvings, circles within circles, and various symbols sprinkled throughout. Meant for spell casting? He noticed what looked like pieces of glass or maybe gems and metal inserts set into it.

John finally stepped inside.

A voice spoke. "He was a genius, but eccentric. A hermit, just like you." It was Husniye's voice. John jumped and spun around. The only thing behind him was Horse, standing in the doorway, staring quizzically at him.

The voice went on. "There are trace amounts of nullstone in the rocks he used for construction. Most mages would avoid it, but Shielken embraced it and used it to quell the natural waves in the aether. Like the shamans of old, he found a way to anchor his spellwork to the aether itself. Hoping to create a stable one-way gate, but he died before he could finish."

"How are you alive?" John gasped.

If Husniye heard him, she gave no indication. "It was perfect bait for me. I stumbled on some of his papers and an old map."

John held up the gatestone, directing his half of the conversation to it. "What should I be doing?"

There was no reply.

211

"I came here for answers. I know that's not the smartest since this is where you were attacked, but …"

Still, silence.

"I just needed something to do, I guess." John finished. Nothing.

"Any other mysterious words of wisdom from beyond the grave? Anything?" With an exasperated sigh, he stepped farther into the room, Olumtahss still in his hand.

Suddenly the stone glowed. So did the floor.

"Ah, Storm." John cursed before everything went black.

⌣

"Have you ever heard of a phylactery?" A voice called John to consciousness, and he floated in a void. In front of him was Husniye. Sort of. John could see her, but when he tried to focus too closely on any detail, things went blurry.

Husniye continued, "What about an Eriminho?"

John looked around, perplexed. He felt like he was trapped in a soap bubble, surrounded by a wall of swirling light. "No," he replied. "Are you dead or alive?"

She smiled. "Yes. Welcome to the aether. Where would you like to go? Somewhere nobody would ever find you?"

He thought for a moment before blurting, "Ece's gatestone."

Husniye laughed heartily. "Choosing you was the right decision."

# 17

John felt like he had just been flung across the world. He staggered, falling into Horse.

He found himself in a massive circular room, its domed roof constructed from beautiful yellow and orange sandstone. Walls carved and painted with patterns stretched up to circular windows near the ceiling, through which light streamed in. Metal rail lines inlaid on the floor led to an enormous doorway. An empty cart, weathered and dull, sat on the line. The lettering above the door read, "Welcome to Wetstone".

To one side, chain mail rattled. "Sir?" A guard stepped forward.

"Sorry, there was a bit of an emergency," John said.

The man nodded, slowly, glancing at the massive white warhorse and taking in its crusty, days-old sword wounds. He stuttered, "Which, ah, house are you?"

"DuFort," John replied without hesitation.

The man stiffened. "Ahh …"

"I said it's an emergency." John quickly mounted and gently nudged Horse, who took a few steps. He couldn't help but smile as the horse lifted his tail and released a pile of shit as they moved. They left the guard staring at the pile.

John rode Horse out of the building like he knew what he was doing, and as they entered the marketplace, throngs of people made way. He grinned. Things looked different from Horse's back. He noticed hats of all kinds, carriages, a boy clinging to a pole like some sort of monkey.

John found a place to dismount near a fruit stall emitting sweet scents. The vendor bowed. "Good morning? You would like some lovely fruit, yes?" He thrust a sample under his nose.

John ignored the man. Taking in the scene, he noticed all eyes were on him. Apparently, strutting through a marketplace on a warhorse was a good way to get noticed. He patted Horse's nose and murmured, "Stay." Then, grabbing his bag, he wandered nonchalantly away from the stall and headed to his destination.

The crowd pressed in around him. He felt the tug of a hand in his pocket, turned, and swung his fist blindly. It connected with something hard, and someone yelled. A ragged child lay at his feet, holding a bloody nose. Several people gasped.

"Sorry," John muttered. He tossed the kid a coin before ducking into the first building he could find—a seed shop, selling all manner of grains and seeds. The upper story housed apartments.

A man on a stool smiled toothlessly. "May I help you sir?"

"I just need to …" John began, then spotted the staircase. "Ah, Got it." He nodded politely before heading straight for the steps.

John did not turn when the man shouted after him, "Where are you going?"

His hand gripped the straps on his bag tight enough to turn the knuckles white, but he kept his voice even as he called back, "Just meeting someone."

At the top of the stairs, a row of rooms lined the wall to his left. These would all be facing the gatestone building he'd just left.

The ancient hardwood floor creaked beneath his weight as he tried every stained, warped door. The first was locked, so was the second. The third opened to reveal a woman in bed, gasping as she held the sheets close against her naked body. "Sorry!" John closed the door and hurried on.

The fourth door was also locked, but the fifth opened into another room just like the previous one. Thankfully, this one was empty. He entered and closed the door behind him before stepping to the window and putting his bag on the bed.

He extracted the new bow and strung it, still pleased at the beauty of the wood. He then selected the arrow with the nullstone arrowhead affixed to it. He balanced the arrow on his finger, then shifted it from hand to hand, testing the weight. He laid it on the windowsill.

John cracked the shutters and peered across at the gatestone building. He gazed at the high windows and caught a glint of light. Glass. He pulled a second arrow from his bag, a warhead. John readied himself, inhaled deeply, nocked the warhead arrow, and released the string. By the time the glass in the opposite window tinkled against the floor, he had the nullstone arrow drawn back. He took another deep breath, then held it, his arm barely moving despite the strain of the bow. He adjusted the arrow, accounting for the ill balance of the nullstone at the tip, and released the weapon. It wobbled, but the fletching held true. The arrow arced through the window with a monstrous cracking sound, followed by a red flash.

As quickly as possible, John unstrung his bow and returned it to the bag, hefted the bag onto his shoulders, and prepared to sprint. At the last second, he stopped and spun to survey the bed. Once well made, the bed was now rumpled from the weight of the bag. John smoothed the blanket, then left the room, leaving no trace of his presence.

As he descended the stairs, he heard more than the typical sounds of the marketplace—louder and more panicked than usual. In the seed shop, the toothless counter clerk was now standing in the doorway, peering into the crowd.

"What happened?" John stepped beside him.

"I don't know." He looked over at John, his eyes narrowing. "Who were you meeting?"

John spoke as he walked by. "They weren't home."

"Who were you—" the man began. John moved quickly out of the merchant's sight and hearing and power-walked through the crowd. As he made his way back to the fruit stall, panic set in in the marketplace.

"Hey, Horse," John called as he approached. The animal nickered at him as if to show that people had given him a wide berth. John spotted patches of blood on the ground. "Trouble, huh?" He slung his bag onto the horse. The horse snorted again.

"Well, I think it's time to get out of here." John mounted and urged Horse into the thinnest part of the crowd. Down the street soldiers with spears approached, marching in formation toward the gatestone building. John went the other way.

After putting some distance between themselves and the market, John led Horse into a deserted alleyway. He fished Olumtahss out of a pants pocket and held it up.

He concentrated before calling out. "Cecil." There was no immediate reply, so he called again. "Cecil."

The voice that responded was not Cecil's, but a less welcome one. "John, it's Ahmet. Listen. I know we got off on the wrong foot...."

John interrupted. "I just broke Ece's gatestone."

"What!"

"The gatekeeper needs to be present to repair the stone, correct?"

"Yes, but you can't be serious. You're messing with me."

"I am not messing with you. If Trey has Ece, he'll have to bring her to the gatestone to fix it, or the Spire will be seriously pissed at him. That's House Husniye's chance to get her back."

"Are you insane?" Ahmet spluttered.

"Maybe," John responded, then cut the connection.

At House Husniye, Cecil and Ahmet stared at each other, each with a hand on the communication stone on the table. "By the aether!" Cecil swore.

Ashen, Ahmet spoke. "He was joking, right? He didn't just ... how would you even do that?"

Cecil pondered. "He might have scratched it with that dagger, I guess."

"Right. Right." Ahmet nodded anxiously, "Nothing to worry about. We have to pay a fine."

As if on cue, Ahu burst into the room. "Ahmet, there is a messenger from the Spire here." She glanced between the two men.

Ahmet combed his hair back with a shaking hand. "I'll ... I'll speak with them."

He scuttled from the room, and Ahu turned to Cecil. "What is going on?"

"John just damaged Ece's gatestone—the one in Wetstone—to force Trey to bring Ece out of hiding."

Ahu barked out a laugh before covering her mouth. "Sorry, I know that's terrible but ..."

"It is pretty ridiculous." He pursed his lips, then moved for the door. "I am going to be a fly on the wall for this."

Cecil caught up with Ahmet at the front door. Hovering in the entry was a large stone orb, carved with runes in a pattern of hoops, swirls, and lines. A glass lens, giving the impression of a floating eye, protruded from the front. Black banners marked with a single line of purple down the center hung from either side. An official Spire messenger.

A voice emanated from the eye. "There has been an incident."

Ahmet nodded. "What happened?"

"Someone struck the Wetstone with a nullstone-tipped arrow. It's damaged. We require Ece to arrive as soon as possible to fix the damage."

"Terrorists from the Storm Church? Was it Sunstone?"

"Possibly, though they rarely target gatestones."

Ahmet demurred. "I thought you had settled things with them."

"No organization has perfect control over its members. Especially the church. Time is of the essence. Please summon Ece. A wagon will arrive shortly."

"Unfortunately, she isn't here."

"Then contact her," the voice snapped.

"She is away on business with Trey. We are having trouble contacting her."

"I don't care for excuses."

"You will have to talk to Trey."

A whirring noise emanated from the eye. "Failure to track the location of your gatekeepers is in violation of our contract."

"I understand. I'm sorry. But you will have to talk to Trey. He is the only one who knows how to reach her."

There were more whirring noises, then the eye ascended, floating upward until it was out of sight. Ahmet sighed, stepped back inside, and closed the door.

Cecil murmured, "So the Spire doesn't know Trey kidnapped Ece?"

Ahmet gave him a sharp glance. "No, they don't know. We are trying to keep it quiet."

Cecil held his hands up. "Sorry."

"Where the hell did he get a nullstone, anyway?" Ahmet spat.

⤺

Trey stood at attention in front of a polished stone. The Spire representative hadn't turned on the visual aspect of the communication stone, so all Trey could see was a pattern. He knew they had a full view of him. Yet another game the Spire liked to play.

A voice came from the stone. "We had a deal, Sir DuFort. No direct interference with the gatestones run by House Husniye."

A huff escaped Trey's lips. "I don't understand you."

"One of House Husniye's gatekeepers is missing."

"You said I could have the house if I helped you get Olumtahss."

"We said we would turn a blind eye to any acquisitions as long as the gatestone network was undisturbed. Kidnapping a gatekeeper, an important one, is crossing a line."

Trey inhaled and exhaled deeply until his panic subsided. "It's a good thing I did, because otherwise Olumtahss would be back into House Husniye's hands. Husniye modified it to only accept Ece to be the next heir, and you failed to recover it."

"That is interesting to know, but my point still stands," the image replied. "This is unacceptable."

Trey hardened his tone. "Ece would never have agreed to an acquisition. I needed her out of the way."

"Again, our concern is not with House Husniye but the rogue stone. We were very clear about this."

Straightening his back, Trey retorted, "Well, since you failed to grab the stone when you had a chance, I'll make sure to hand it over once I take control of House Husniye." Trey continued, more sarcastically. "Does that sound acceptable to you?"

"Ece's gatestone has been damaged."

Trey started. "What?"

"We need her at her stone immediately so she can perform repairs."

Trey nodded. "Of course."

"We do not want any delays. Every hour it's down costs a fortune."

Scrambling to make things right, Trey took his tone down a notch. "Of course, I'll take care of it right away."

"Be sure that you do."

The connection cut off, and Trey kicked the chair next to him, cursing loudly.

⸻

"Hello, Trey." Ece greeted Trey as he opened the door. He shot her a predatory smile. She waved, rattling her chains. Covered in a thin layer of grime, Ece's tattered clothes did little to hide her body. A stench emanated from the cell.

Trey loomed over her. "How do you like your new clothes?"

"It reminds me of that old play. The one where the princess dressed up as a peasant to seduce what's his name? Because his father forbade any fraternization between their houses? What was that called again?" Ece appeared thoughtful.

Trey's smile faltered as she continued. "There was that scene when he bosses her around and she realizes that, well, he's kind of a dick. For the life of me, I can't remember the name. She ends up with the serving boy though."

Trey stared at her, jaw clenched as she gave him a sweet smile. "It made quite the splash. I believe your father may

221

have banned it. Full of rather clever social commentary. Much of it still applies. I quite liked it."

She gave him a sidelong look and asked, "Speaking of, how does your conquest of my house go? Any luck so far?" Trey lost patience.

"Enough," Trey finally said. "You are coming with me."

"Ah, he can speak. You know, the silent glare only works when someone's scared of you."

In a flash, Trey's sword was in his hand, through the bars of the cell, and against Ece's neck. "Really. You aren't afraid of me? I killed Maria. I killed Husniye. I have removed House Husniye as a player. You have lost. I have all the cards."

"I suppose it's because all your strength was stolen, not earned. It's hard to be afraid of a man who ..." Trey flicked the sword and cut her cheek. Ece hissed with pain but went on. "Can't even keep up with the most basic of political discussions, and instead rely on—"

"Shut the fuck up!" Trey screamed.

"—brute force to achieve anything. That's why I am not afraid of you."

Trey, agitated, paused, composed himself, then left. "Put her in the wagon," he barked to the two guards as he passed.

Behind him, Trey heard Ece laugh.

# 18

"John, are you ready?" Cecil asked. John gripped the stone.

"Ready as I'll ever be, I suppose."

"All right. I am coming through first. Can you feel the connection?"

"Yes," John said.

"Are you sure?" Cecil asked. "This is the first time you are moving something through a gate."

"I think Husniye put some spells on it to make it easier," John said. "Also, this isn't my first time. You came through. So did Li and all the pallbearers, and Obi visited me."

"Oh, Obi came by and said hi? Nice guy. Bit of an oddball though. Loves to travel."

"So how is this different?" John asked.

"Well, every other time someone was pushing. This time you are pulling. Does that make sense?"

"Why can't you just push through, like before?" John asked the stone.

"Normally when you travel, there are two gatekeepers. One pushes, the other pulls. Without both gatekeepers, it becomes difficult. Think of it like dragging a heavy load without wheels. It took almost twenty mages pushing from the other side to move all the pallbearers through.

"Almost twenty." John tried to calculate how much it would cost to hire that many mages.

"Wait," John said. "How did you get through? While drunk?" There was a pause. John felt panic leak through the connection.

"Ehh, it just worked out?"

"It worked out? Did you hire a group of mages to push you?"

"In truth, it was chaotic. A bunch of mages and people were trying to push through the gatestone, and I just sort of … well, I just … slipped in."

"You snuck up to the gatestone while a bunch of mages were trying to get to me and managed to slip through?"

"Husniye taught me a few tricks. There was a lot of chaos. There is a gatestone in the basement attuned to Olumtahss and while everyone was milling around, I just drew a spellcircle in the corner of the room and sort of hijacked the connection."

"Then how did you get back?"

"I actually don't know," Cecil said. "I was wondering about that myself. Anyway, enough chat. Al-Haytham is pushing on this side, so I need you to do your gatekeeper thing and try to pull me through."

"All right," John said. "What does "attuned to Olumtahss" mean?"

"Oh, there is a way to make certain gatestones work better with certain other gatestones. Don't worry about it."

"Right. Let me try this." John closed his eyes.

In his mind, he imagined a bridge disappearing into the fog. A vague shape formed in the distance. John reached toward it. A shining suit of armor came forward, with bloody tears coming out of the visor. John sighed internally and pulled.

"Uh, hey," Cecil said.

John blinked until his vision came back, staring up at the blue sky. "That felt like I just got punched," John said.

"From what I hear it's pretty tough," Cecil said. He shifted uncomfortably. "So, uh," Cecil muttered, staring up at the sky.

"You have orders to arrest me and drag me back to Husniye, right?" John asked.

"Oh. Well, basically." Cecil said, looking relieved.

"This is the only chance we have at getting Ece back and fixing this," John stated.

"I know, but Ahmet made a deal with the Spire. If we turn Olumtahss over to the Spire, House Husniye will continue to exist, to some extent at least. And if we lose Olumtahss here, the house has no chance."

"I suppose Ahmet gets to stay as permanent head of the house, right?"

"I suppose he will."

"That's convenient for him."

"Please just come with me, and let's go back," Cecil said, then paused a moment. "Wait. Can't you tell what someone's motivation is when they try to move through your gatestone? Why did you let me through if you knew I was here to drag you back to House Husniye?" Cecil accused.

John smiled. "Husniye said you were an idiot. So let's be idiots together." He stared down Cecil.

"And how the hell are we supposed to win?" Cecil asked after a long moment.

"How many men do you think Trey will bring with him? I don't know much, but I do know that the Spire hates it when one of their gatestones goes down. He will be in a hurry.

"Even if he doesn't bring many, he would still bring some," Cecil countered. "Right now, we have you and me."

"We can ambush them. I have armor-piercing arrows. I can pick them off and you can deal with the rest."

"That's ... I mean, that is a plan. I don't know if it would work."

"Can we move more soldiers through the gatestone in uh ..." John trailed off, realizing he didn't actually know where he was.

"No, that would tip Trey off, and it would break our contract with the Spire if we started moving soldiers through the gate network."

"Oh, right. I read that in the book. Could we move them in secret?"

"Probably not."

"You mentioned mercenaries earlier," John said.

"Yeah, we could hire some, but House Husniye is broke right now. Maybe we can scrape together some money. John, this is stupid. We have almost no chance of winning."

"You could even say it's idiotic." John smirked.

Cecil inhaled, then released a heavy sigh. "Fine. Let's be idiots." He broke into a grin.

"Well?" Ahmet stared at al-Haytham, who sat cross-legged in front of a large, red crystal sprouting from the ground like a massive bush. A lamp hung from the ceiling overhead, giving the basement room a red glow and illuminating a long wall of cabinets. Each of the thousand tiny drawers was labeled. The rest of the room was scattered with strange stone furniture and miscellaneous bookcases.

Al-Haytham placed a hand gently on the crystal. "One moment, please." He gave a small chuckle. "It seems that Cecil is having trouble convincing John to cooperate."

"We don't need him to cooperate. Just drag him back to Wetstone, wait for the gate to be fixed, and send him through."

"And what if John runs off into the woods, hmm?" Al-Haytham asked.

"That better be hypothetical." Ahmet howled, jowls shaking.

"It would be nice to send more help. Do we have any local resources?"

"The Spire has agents swarming the area because of the damaged gatestone." Ahmet's voice rose on the last two words. "If they get wind that we're involved, the house is doomed."

"Well, we might have to hire mercenaries."

Ahmet cursed loudly, slapping his thigh. "Why is nothing easy?"

"There are still some communication stones in Wetstone, including one at a bank. We could open a line of credit. Do I have your permission to look into that?"

"Fine, permission granted. But we are already racking up debt."

"I have some extra funds I stored away for emergencies."

"Why didn't you mention that earlier?"

Al-Haytham said, "Well, I was saving it for emergencies."

Ahmet responded with a glare.

Al-Haytham continued. "I'll take care of this. Don't worry."

Ahmet grunted, then stood up. "I hope you do. Let me know if anything changes. And try not to spend too much." He stomped out of the room.

Al-Haytham waited until he was out of earshot, then turned to Ahu. "Do me a favor. Could you grab whatever coin we have left in the vault, and Cecil's armor?"

She gave al-Haytham a look. "Why would Cecil need full armor to catch a man running around in the woods?"

Al-Haytham gave her a slight grin. "Let's just say Cecil is being an idiot again, and this time he has a partner."

She burst into laughter and nodded. "I'll see what I can scrape together."

"My personal stash was under my bed last time I checked. If you could grab that too, I would be grateful. Oh, and Yeela too. We need to track Ece's movement."

Ahu clapped her hands in excitement. "I'll see what I can do."

A few minutes later, Ahu returned with Yeela following, reluctant, confused, and complaining, "What's going on?"

"Do you still have that spellstone that lets you track Ece?" al-Haytham asked.

Yeela rolled her eyes. "Of course I do."

"Do you know the accuracy? The error margins?"

"Well, it was designed so I could find her on Hydra Island, so probably not too accurate at much distance."

Al-Haytham stroked his beard, eyebrows furrowed in thought. "We need to move you to a closer gate then, so you can tell us exactly where Trey is."

"How would that help? It's designed to track Ece, not Trey," Yeela said, but al-Haytham was already pulling out maps, muttering to himself.

Ahu gently patted Yeela's shoulder. "John, the current gatekeeper of Olumtahss, damaged the gatestone in Wetstone. Trey is on the way with Ece now, and we are planning to try to intercept them."

Yeela held a hand up to her mouth, but her grin was still visible. "He didn't. Oh, she is so proud of that gatestone too. It's the only one there." Yeela's grin grew wider. "There is no way the other idiots there would be able to fix it if something happened. They are all spoiled brats who wanted a title. That's amazing."

Al-Haytham broke in, thrusting a map into Yeela's face. "Here. Go here and get on a communication stone. Here is some coin." He pushed them, clinking, into Yeela's hands. "Let us know exactly where Ece is."

"Like, right now?"

"Yes. Now. Get on a comm stone as soon as you can."

"I guess I'll get going." Yeela backed away.

Al-Haytham turned his gaze to the pile of armor and weapons at Ahu's feet. "We need to get the rest of this to the gatestone in the basement as soon as possible."

"I just saw Ahmet head down there. Do we tell him?"

"Absolutely not."

From the doorway, Yeela called. "Is this a secret operation then?"

Al-Haytham pointed without looking. "Yes, now go!"

"Righty-o" Yeela sang, waving goodbye.

Ahu snapped her fingers. "I can put his things in the dumbwaiter, then smuggle them to the gatestone in a tea cart. Could you send them through without anybody noticing?"

Al-Haytham grunted. "I will do my best."

Ahmet shook the man's hand furiously. "Thank you so much for coming on such short notice."

"Of course." The man shook back far less enthusiastically. He was dressed in Spire colors, the official badge on his chest.

From behind the tea cart, al-Haytham and Ahu watched the flurry of activity around the basement room. The tea and snacks Ahu had placed on top had already been snapped up. Now they both casually moved toward the gatestone as Ahmet finally released the official's hand and bowed, saying, "I hope to resolve this situation amicably, without any farther drama or bloodshed."

The Spire representative returned the bow. "Of course."

"Let's head up to my office." He motioned to the man to proceed him. As he passed Ahu, Ahmet snatched the last plate of baklava on the cart. She gave her best smile as she continued to roll it right up to the stone.

Al-Haytham leaned on the stone, furrowing his brow as he concentrated on the items Ahu had concealed inside the cart.

The voice of a young servant broke in. "Sir, we could use your help. We still have a few things to move through, and the current mages are already tapped." Ahu held her breath as the boy leaned closer. "Spire folk always are a pain to move, for some reason."

Al-Haytham's brow was beaded with sweat, but he smiled at the boy as the cloth fluttered. Ahu felt its weight change as the hidden armor, weapons, and coins vanished. Al-Haytham stepped away from the stone.

"What do you need me to do?"

Cecil patted Horse on the nose, smiling. "I was wondering where Snow got off to." Cecil paused. "What are you calling him?"

John looked a bit embarrassed. "Horse."

"Really?"

"I just ... it fit. It's a horse."

"It is. A very horsey horse."

"Shut up," John muttered. "Want some lunch?"

"Sure."

Cecil watched with growing amazement as John produced a veritable feast of fruit, venison, and bread from his bag. "Where did you get all this food? I thought you were hiding out in the woods, starving."

"Obi visited me. And I hunted."

"Obi gave you food? That was nice of him."

"Yeah." John took a bite of venison, gesturing for Cecil to do the same. They sat in silence for some time, eating, while Horse munched on some grass nearby.

Cecil broke the silence first. "I'm sorry about your friend."

John winced. "It's ... not fine. Not yet. But I think it will be, eventually. Hold on, al-Haytham is back." He grabbed the stone around his neck and concentrated. "He has Yeela with him and your kit. They are heading to the gatestone in the basement."

"Fantastic! How many mages does he have pushing?"

"I think it's just al-Haytham."

Cecil made a face. "Oh."

"One moment." John shut his eyes. The armor appeared in a faint cloud of sparkles, then clanked as it hit the ground, along with a bag. John keeled over, gagging.

Cecil was at his side immediately, patting his back. "I know, it's tough. You are doing a great job."

John managed to swallow. "I don't want to waste food."

Cecil burst out laughing, rubbing his back. "It's all good."

"Give me a moment. Al-Haytham is triangulating where Ece is coming from."

Cecil nodded. "Of course." He went to his things, taking stock. "No halberd. Ask al-Haytham if they could send it through."

John coughed, looking up. "He says it was too big to smuggle in. You'll have to use your sword."

"Damn. All right," Cecil muttered.

After finishing lunch, John and Cecil strolled down the road, Horse clopping alongside them. The road dipped down into the flood valley of the river at their left. Horse's footsteps kicked up orange dust that drifted lazily in the still air.

On its other side, the river was bounded by a sheer cliff, carved away by the water over many years. To their right was farmland, stretching across the flood valley until it hit another cliff.

"He is on the same route, right?" Cecil asked.

John didn't even bother grabbing the stone. "Al-Haytham said they would update us, and Yeela said if we keep asking, she would castrate me. So no news is good news."

Cecil chuckled. "Ece really knows how to pick them."

They paused in front of a group of farmers digging the sediment from a ditch. They nodded hello as the two men passed, and John called out. "Hello, sir. Does your valley often flood?"

One man lifted the brim of his straw, unsure how to respond to John's unusual greeting. At last, he replied, "From time to time."

"So you can't use the road while it's flooded?" John asked.

The man leaned on his shovel. "We built it up to make sure it's still passable when we flood the fields."

John blinked. "You flood the fields on purpose?"

Cecil broke in. "They are growing water drops. It's a delicacy. They need to flood the field as part of the growth cycle."

The farmer nodded. "Aye. The plants need to be flooded or the fruits dry up."

John looked farther down the road. In the distance, a brown structure was vaguely visible. He nodded toward it. "That the dam?"

"Aye."

"You close it when you want the fields to flood."

"Aye."

"And the road never gets flooded when you do that?"

"We're careful."

"But it could flood?" John insisted.

"I suppose," the man admitted, shrugging.

"Right, thanks." John resumed walking.

After they'd gone beyond the farmers' hearing, Cecil leaned in. "What are you thinking? Of flooding Trey out?"

"Maybe. If we can make them stop, I can pick them off with arrows." He avoided Cecil's frown, focusing on the dam. It was like a giant wooden door, currently open, letting the river flow past.

At the foot of the dam, John placed his hand on the base. "How do you open it again once you close it? Wouldn't the water pressure keep it shut?" He looked down at the gate in the water, parallel to the river bank. A giant log formed the top of the gate, tarred to prevent rotting. The log was far longer than the door, extending a distance beyond the hinge. He answered his own question. "Leverage. Plus ..." He leaned over the edge and saw something like a handle atop the gate. John grabbed it and lifted, grunting. It rose slightly. He dropped it, and with a dull thud, the wooden slat fell back into place. "They can adjust how much water goes through with these slats."

Cecil nodded. "Right, so they close the gate, then adjust with those slats. They probably have to release all the water to open it again."

"This gate is lower than the level of the road, though. I don't think we could flood it from here."

Cecil pointed upriver. "What about the bridge?"

John's head snapped up. "If the field is flooded, and the bridge is gone, then they would be trapped on three sides. River on the left, flooded field on the right, and no bridge in front.... And, wait, I have an idea. Let's talk to al-Haytham."

As it emerged from the stone in John's hand, al-Haytham's voice was overlaid with the sound of rustling paper. "I can't find the dam on any of our maps, but I believe you. There is a cliff nearby that John can set up on, but how will you get to them, Cecil?"

"I have a mudwalker stone. I can cross the river with that."

"Those are designed to let you navigate mud, not walk on water."

"They work on water."

"How do you know that?"

Cecil paused before trying. "I just do?"

"Cecil."

"Okay, remember that swampy shithole those bandits were hiding in, and we had a pile of mudwalker stones? I played around with them after the fighting was done, figured out that they let you walk on water, but only for a little bit before they failed."

"I also remember you claimed you used all the very expensive mudwalker stones during that deployment."

"It was only a few leftovers."

A long, low sigh came from al-Haytham. "Cecil, I helped raise you."

Cecil caved. "Fine. We had a bunch left over and had a contest to see who could run the farthest across a lake."

As John cackled, al-Haytham released another sigh. "So you have one with you?"

"Yes, in my pack. I always carry one with me."

"So your plan is John waits above on overwatch and Cecil charges across the water to ambush them?"

"Yes."

"Risky."

Cecil and John exchanged glances. John spoke first. "We know."

"Good luck."

# 19

Cecil and John lay behind a bush at the top of the cliff, nestled among leaves, peering at the men below. Cecil wore his full armor, blackened with mud to avoid reflected sunlight giving away their position.

"Trey's not there," John said bitterly. Cecil grunted, and they watched three scouts in DuFort colors talking into communication stones.

Cecil held out his hand. "Give me Olumtahss. Let me contact al-Haytham quickly."

John rolled over to fish out the stone. "Why can't you use yours?"

"It's too far." Holding the red gem to his mouth, Cecil said, "Al-Haytham, we have a problem. He sent a scout ahead."

"Of course he did. One moment." Al-Haytham sounded exhausted. They winced at the squeal of feedback, then al-Haytham. "Yeela, are you there?"

"Yeah, I'm here." Her voice came through the stone.

"Is Trey …?"

"He's still on the same road, still moving, hasn't stopped." There was a pause, then a muffled exchange: "I know there is a line, this is an emergency. I have to stay on the … I don't care. Here, take another coin and get out. I need privacy, okay?"

Cecil and John exchanged glances. Cecil asked, "Is Yeela at a public communication stone?"

She snapped, "Yes, I am. Please hurry this up."

Cecil frowned. "Why hasn't Trey stopped?"

Al-Haytham snorted. "He's already running late. We expected him hours ago. I don't know if he has time to make a detour."

Yeela interjected, "Tell me about it, they really don't like one person being on a stone for this long. Wish the bastard would hurry up."

A short while later, the main body of Trey's entourage came into view. When the rear guard finally appeared, Cecil reached for the stone around John's neck. Without taking his eyes from the road, he spoke. "Al-Haytham. It's more than we thought."

"How many?"

Cecil paused to count. "At least thirty."

Al-Haytham was silent.

Squinting, John added, "Only five in DuFort colors that I can see, not including Trey. Plus the three scouts. I see some crossbowmen too."

Al-Haytham sighed, "Ah, that's why he's so late. He was organizing a militia escort."

Cecil pounded the ground with his fist.

Trey leaned from the carriage to stare down the road at the skeleton of the bridge, temper rising. "Scouts, cross the river," he barked. "Look for ambushes on the other side. You men, find something to fix the bridge, or find wherever the bridge went. Now. And keep these fools in formation!"

His men scrambled, yelling orders and corralling the militia who had already started scooping water from the swollen river with their helmets.

"You." He turned to glare at the warlock. "Do something."

The man grinned up at him. "Problem is, this carriage is designed to make any magic cast fail. How else are you supposed to keep a mage locked up?" He kicked the iron-rimmed wheel and tittered.

"Figure something out," Trey said. "Move some rocks to make a new bridge." He watched his personal guard moving among the militia, like sheepdogs guiding a flock, forcing the men back into a semblance of formation. In the distance, his scouts picked their way across the bridge frame, arms out for balance as they walked across the railings. He leaned against the bars of the cage, sighing. They were trapped on three sides—the river to the left, flooded fields on the right, and in front of them, a damaged bridge. They were at a disadvantage, but at least they couldn't be easily attacked. His men had already arranged most of their makeshift force behind the wagon, forming a shield as they waited. Trey glanced up to the clifftop on the other side of the river, then sighed again.

As John angrily fiddled with an arrow, al-Haytham's voice came through the stone. "We tried, that's the important thing."

"Just let me put an arrow in him."

Cecil turned and stared at John. "Into Trey? I don't know if that's an option."

"Right, because that would anger the Spire?"

"John, calm down," al-Haytham said gently. "There isn't really anything we can do."

"They found the bridge boards," Cecil announced, watching the scouts carrying them back. "They still can't figure out how to open the dam though, so that's fun."

"Great," John snarled. So I guess we just watch them leave?"

Cecil patted John on the shoulder. "We should fall back. They haven't spotted us yet."

⁓

Trey's jaw clenched and his knuckles tightened on his communication stone. The Spire representative's voice was still lecturing, and behind him the warlock giggled. He again apologized; meanwhile, three men dropped a plank into the river. Thankfully, the Spire representative signed off, and he dropped the stone back into his pocket.

"You know, we could take Ece out of the wagon and walk across," the warlock said.

"Not taking that chance," Trey spat. Ece laughed behind him, and he turned to glare at her.

That's when the yelling started.

Trey's head jerked around to the road, where water had bubbled over the embankment. Trey groaned. "One of you deal with that dam, now!" he screamed, grabbing the reins of the horses.

⁓

"We should start falling back. They haven't spotted us yet," Cecil said quietly.

Yelling echoed up to their position. John gave a gleeful laugh. "The road is flooding! This part is low enough to flood!"

Together they watched two of Trey's men, a handful of militias behind them, sprint to the dam and seize the gate, trying to release the pressure, but everything had mysteriously seized up and stopped moving. On the road, Trey sat on the driver's seat of the prison carriage, whipping the horses, trying to get the carriage to turn.

John shifted, drawing an arrow toward the bow in his hand.

Cecil muttered, "Don't. He doesn't have enough room to turn it around without going into the water. Don't give us away yet."

John glanced over to his side with a quizzical expression. "Yet?"

"Let's see how this goes."

The water crept onto the road. Trey's angry voice echoed through the valley. Most of the militiamen milled around, some even splashing each other in the rising water. Trey's own guard, those dressed in vivid blue, were either trying to fix the bridge for the wagon or staring at the rising water. They'd turned the carriage perpendicular to the road, but the horses refused to move it farther.

A bright light, probably from a flashstone, flared near the dam and there was a shout of warning. Then, with a crash, the dam broke, releasing a furious gush of water, scattering wood shards in every direction.

"Huh," Cecil said, looking downstream, then cracked a smile. "I guess Trey's men figured out how to open the dam."

The water whipped down the channel, sweeping the feet from under the soldiers standing on the road.

"Whoa," John said, "The farmers aren't going to like this." John glanced across the field, where the farmers they paid off were hiding and watching. They all stood, one angrily waving his arms.

The advancing water stripped flagstones from the road, creating a deep gouge, turning a muddy brown as it churned through the soil. The carriage slid sideways toward the river.

"This is working much better than our plan," Cecil said, watching the chaos unfold. "I think it's probably good to start now."

"Right." John knelt and nocked an arrow. Cecil reached for the stone around John's neck to report, "We are moving in," then kicked a rope down the cliff and slid down.

John waited for someone to notice them. He heard al-Haytham shouting through the stone, but didn't engage. Trey had already abandoned the driver's seat of the wagon, and was out of sight, as was the warlock. John clicked his tongue, scanning the chaos.

Below him, Cecil reached the bottom of the hill. He already had the mudstone in hand; light flashed, and a glowing rectangle stretched across the raging river before him. He took one step forward, but the waves ripped the fragile magic to pieces, like paper in a storm. He stopped short, stuck on the wrong side of the river. Just then, Trey's men noticed him. John swore. "Ah shit." A militia crossbowman loaded his crossbow by pulling it back with a goat's hook.

John loosed an arrow, and the crossbowmen fell with a scream, the arrow piercing his lung. Cecil gestured back to him that he could not reach Trey.

John pulled out another arrow.

By now, the alarm had gone across the valley, and everyone scrambled. Trey's men tried to cross, but the swift water drove them back. Another crossbowman fell to John's arrow, and the rest rushed for cover behind their allies' shields or the wagon.

Jon pulled out another arrow.

A bang and a blinding flash of light left John blinking. Below, he could see a smoking hole near Cecil's feet, armor lit with a pattern of glowing runes had absorbed most of the magical blast. Trey's forces weren't the only ones with offensive spellstones. Cecil raised his arm, and the ground on the other side of the newly formed gorge exploded upwards showering Trey's forces with water and chunks of rock. John heard commanders shouting. One officer tried to cross the bridge supports and get back to the main group. John took a breath and loosed another arrow. It pierced the target's neck, and he fell with a splash into the raging water. The others swarmed for cover, using the bridge planks like shields.

John pulled out another arrow.

Several militiamen had already made a break for it, sprinting away from the fighting. Behind the wagon, Trey's guards struggled to don their armor, which spilled from an open chest strapped to the back of the wagon. One fell to an arrow to the chest. The rest grabbed whatever armor they could, then dove behind the now crowded wagon. Another light flashed, then a bang.

John pulled out another arrow.

Now the crossbowmen returned fire. A crossbow bolt whizzed by John's head and another thudded into the ground in front of him. Trey's men, shooting from the cover of the shields, made them hard targets. John spotted Cecil on a small patch of ground between the cliff and the river. Now, a sitting duck, he tried to make himself as small a target as possible. John, however, was now the primary focus. He took aim, and another man fell.

John pulled out another arrow.

Now the rear guard from House DuFort organized, ordering the remaining militia to form up, create a semblance of a shield wall for the crossbowmen. John hit an officer in the chest. He stumbled. The militia broke and ran. From the corner of his left eye, John caught a white blur streaming past and the sound of hooves, but he stayed focused. He pulled out another arrow as a man scrambled atop the wagon. John loosed the arrow at him, but it veered sideways, flying harmlessly off into the field. The man smiled up at him, an unsettling grin, and laughed. Around him, the air seemed to shimmer. Black fog materialized and spread from his body like miniature thunderclouds, complete with lightning flashes.

"Storm!" The cry went up, and what remained of Trey's auxiliary forces collapsed. John watched as one militia crossbowman threw down his crossbow, then leaped across the gorge to safety. But in the next moment, a voice boomed out, "I see you, hunter!"

It was the man atop the wagon. The dark, almost violet clouds coalesced before him—a massive thing, with dark wings and silver talons formed on the road. Its body was primarily smoke. Next came a whisper, but louder than a thunderclap, the word: "Seek!" The bird took to the air.

On the ground, Cecil fumbled for his communication stone. "John!" he yelled.

John saw Horse slide to a halt beside Cecil. John wasn't sure how Horse ended up in the valley; Horse was always unpredictable. He snatched up his own stone. "Take out Trey," he ordered. He released Olumtahss to snatch up another arrow as the smoke creature loomed in the sky above him.

It dove, and John's arrow passed through its body. John rolled to the side, his quiver bouncing away and the arrows scattering across the hillside. The creature demolished the patch of ground where he had just knelt. Stone exploded and John coughed in the dust cloud. He checked his bow, gently tugging the string, before glancing up at the bird. The creature was wheeling about, diving, eyes and talons shining against the black Storm of a body. John hefted his bow, pulled his last arrow back, and waited. The being leveled off, heading straight for him.

John loosed the arrow.

The arrow hit the creature in the eye, and there was a sound like a thousand vases shattering. The creature slammed into the ground in a cloud of smoke. John raised an arm to shield his face, waiting for the dust to settle. He nearly missed seeing a single eye, surrounded by wisps of fog, float in front of him. John whipped out his knife just as it lunged toward him. His knifepoint met the glowing white orb in its center, and it shattered. Everything went black.

Cecil watched as the hillside erupted in smoke. He grimaced, then patted Horse's neck. He didn't see enough space for the horse to make a running start, so ruled out fording the river. But Horse didn't need running room. He made a gravity-defying leap across the angry water and landed them on the hostile bank. Cecil loosened his white-knuckle grip from Horse's mane, took a breath, then pulled his sword. Horse surged forward, and Cecil made an awkward slash at a DuFort guard, who ducked and dove for a spear that a militiaman had dropped.

Cecil swung from the saddle, half falling and half leaping toward the man, twisting his body so the spearpoint skittered off his chest plate, bringing his sword down. The man tried to back up, but the sword caught his collarbone, and he fell with a cry.

The others organized quickly and swarmed in Cecil's direction. One charged, sword extended, opposite hand gripping the middle of the blade to better control the point. The method was a good way to grapple and dive into gaps in armor. Cecil raised his sword above his head as if he intended to crash it down onto the other man's head. The reaction was just what Cecil had wanted, the man raised his sword to catch Cecil's and drive his point into the gap at Cecil's neck. Instead, Cecil snapped his sword to the side, catching the man's wrist and severing the sword hand.

As Cecil caught his breath, another man stepped forward. This one had donned his armor in the chaos. Cecil saluted him, he saluted back, and they took their stances.

# 20

"Well, Hunter, you certainly know how to get into messes."

Wearily, John said, "Hello Husniye."

"This was a nasty spell. If it weren't for me, your skin would have just melted off."

"Thanks," John said. He almost sounded sincere.

"Watch the sarcasm, boy. It's not a good habit to get into."

John stared at her, nonplussed.

"And don't talk back either."

"I didn't say any—"

"You thought it. Now, back to the real world. Do help Cecil out. He's having a bit of trouble."

John woke with a gasp. He groaned as he made his way to his feet. In the valley, the militia had fled, but Trey's men had managed to regroup around the wagon. Cecil continued the struggle, Horse at his side bleeding from new wounds. Multiple dead or wounded men lay at his feet. Two men, each in full armor, menaced them with polearms. The warlock, the one who had sent the bird, waved from the top of the wagon. Wisps of Storm floated about him.

John scanned the ground, spotted a few of the arrows that had fallen out of his quiver, and grabbed them up. He took aim at the warlock. Again, the arrow veered to the side.

"You!" A voice carried on the wind. The warlock glared at him as he nocked and loosed another arrow. More Storm clouds gathered around the warlock, and laughter echoed in the air, as this arrow, too, went astray. John took a breath, pulled out another arrow, then another. Each time, they veered off to the right, and John studied their flight path.

John aimed far to the left and let an arrow fly. It veered to the right, zipping by the warlock's head with a hiss. The man scrambled off the wagon, Storm clouds swirling wildly and scattering.

John couldn't get a good shot into the melee and didn't want to hit Cecil. He had no choice but to descend. He shouldered his quiver and scooped up whatever arrows he could see. Seizing the rope Cecil had used earlier, John scrambled down, slipping and sliding as he went. He managed to get across the rapidly diminishing river without getting his bow wet, holding it above his head as he stumbled through the cold water.

With the smoke from the flashstones dissipating, John emerged from the river. In the distance, he heard Trey's voice. Cecil, still facing off against his two armored foes, bled from a wound. A trail of crimson wound down his arm and dripped to the ground. John raised his bow and shot one man in the foot, where he wore no armor.

The man fell, cursing, and Cecil charged the other, swinging his sword wildly. The guard didn't take the bait, but raised a war hammer longer than Cecil's sword, allowing him to keep Cecil at bay. He made small shifts, trying to bait Cecil into a mistake, and positioning his body to keep Cecil between John and himself.

John kneeled, eyes locked on the two pair of feet visible behind the wagon. He glanced down at his quiver. Two more arrows. He took aim, holding the bow awkwardly sideways so it could be low enough to the ground, and released one arrow.

The first arrow hit someone's heel, and as that person fell to the ground, John sent the second into the exposed chest. The face, visible between the wheels belonged to the warlock.

"Was hoping for Trey," John muttered as he stood. He grabbed a spear and moved toward Cecil. The weapon felt awkward, unfamiliar, but Horse stepped to his side and advanced with him.

Before them, Cecil switched his grip midswing, grasping the blade in his hand and hooking the warhammer with the crossguard. He yanked, hoping to disarm the guard. It didn't work. The soldier flicked Cecil's sword to the side, then swung at his head. He did not, however, expect Cecil to let go of the sword and tackle him, freeing the dagger from his side. Before the other man could react, Cecil poked the point into the eye slit of the helmet. "Yield!" Cecil shouted. The man cursed and let the warhammer fall, and John breathed a sigh of relief.

Together, John and Cecil eyed the wagon, which listed dangerously toward the water at the side of the road. Cecil called, "Ece? Are you all right in there?"

A laugh rose from the interior. "Quite all right. Thanks for the show." She appeared behind the bars of the door and leaned against them. She was skinny and filthy but otherwise appeared unharmed.

John remembered the second pair of boots he had seen on the other side, and he shouted, "Trey, why don't you come out?"

Trey stepped out from behind the wheel, hands raised. He glanced toward the door, and from the other side of the bars, Ece smirked at him. Suddenly, Trey turned. His rapier hissed out of the scabbard, and he lunged at her heart.

John and Cecil, defenseless, yelled in unison, "No!"

As the point of the weapon approached her chest, the rapier rusted and fell to dust. Trey glanced as his empty hand with an expression of disbelief.

"I know a few tricks," Ece said.

Trey cursed and raised his hands again. Sourly, he looked to Cecil and John. "You got me."

It was Cecil who noticed Trey's eyes fixed on Olumtahss, dangling around John's neck. Cautiously, he said, "Ece, we need to get you to Wetstone. Then maybe we can all go back to House Husniye and sort things out."

While John busied himself repositioning his bow and quiver, Trey broke into a sprint.

Cecil made a grab, but Trey skipped past and headed straight toward John, closing in fast. The knife he pulled from his belt arced with silver light.

John whipped out his knife and countercharged. Trey thrust, but John knocked the blade to the side and shoved him to the ground. As Trey struggled to rise, John jumped on top of him. He forced the arm with the knife aside, then slid his own knife into Trey's upper chest. Trey gurgled and grabbed weakly at John before collapsing.

Cecil rushed forward. "Are you okay? Sorry, he got by me."

John stood up, glancing at a trickle of blood on his forearm. "It's fine."

They stared at Trey's body for a moment.

"You know, the Spire really doesn't like it when you kill gatekeepers," Cecil said.

"Right." John strode toward the wagon. "This is yours. I name you my heir and abdicate my position as gatekeeper." He yanked Olumtahss from his neck and tossed the stone at Ece. Her manacles rattled as she raised a hand to catch it.

"Thank you kindly, sir," Ece replied. "Now, would you mind grabbing the keys?"

The keys were located on the warlock's body, and Cecil helped Ece find something to cover herself. They then set about arranging triage for the wounded among the remaining militiamen and guards. With Trey's death, the fight had gone out of them.

Suddenly, a voice rose over the groans of the wounded, screaming, "What did you do?"

The farmer was standing in the still ankle-high water of his field. Chunks of plants floated past him, ripped up by the force of the water zipping past. A few other men trudged toward them across the field, wielding pitchforks and billhooks, a machete-like tool with a curve at the end.

Between bites of Cecil's ration bar, Ece said, "Oh my."

"Cecil, just pay them off," John said.

Cecil turned to him. "We already gave them a lot of money."

"Yeah, to remove the bridge and jam the dam closed. Not to have the dam and their fields destroyed." John checked his arm for range of motion and winced. Now that the fighting had stopped, the pain set in.

"Well, that's fair enough," Cecil said. He turned to the farmers as they scrambled up on the road.

The man pointed at the chaos. "What the hell happened?"

"They blew up the dam."

"No shit!" he said. "You ruined our entire crop!"

"Listen Mr. … uhhh …" Cecil began.

"Pulou," the man supplied.

"Pulou, I admit things got out of hand."

"You don't say."

"But we are willing to pay for the damage," Cecil said. There was a moment's pause.

"That so?" Pulou said, and the farmers seemed to relax.

"We'll also need a cart back to Wetstone," Cecil said. Pulou stepped up close to Cecil, and a whispered conversation ensued. Eventually, Cecil nodded at Pulou and walked over to his pack, shuffling through the coins. He returned to Pulou with a large bag of coins. Pulou looked through it, nodded, and began shouting across the field for someone to bring the wagon around, and reinstall the bridge.

"That was perhaps one of the most expensive wagon rides I have ever had," Cecil grumbled.

Ece, having left a small puddle of drool on Cecil's shoulder as she slept, smiled at him disarmingly. "I think it was worth it. Now, let us get home." Ece walked into the building housing the gatestone.

A large man, wearing jewelry and a sporting beard, approached. "Ece, thank the gods you are here. Here." He handed Ece a strange disk with symbols on it.

Ece held up the disk, looking confused. "What, uh?"

The man returned her confusion. "To repair the gatestone?" Ece turned and looked at Cecil, questions on her face.

"Did Trey not mention where you were going?" Cecil asked.

Ece turned to the man and said, "One moment." She walked over to Cecil. The two of them had a quick, whispered conversation, ending when Cecil pointed at John, and Ece burst out laughing.

Ece left with the man. "Wait here, hopefully this won't take too much time."

"If you need to rest more—" Cecil began, but Ece cut him off.

"I'll be fast. Let's just get home.

"All right," Cecil said. John slumped up against a wall and waited, the exhaustion of the day catching up to him. They both sat in silence, occasionally cracking jokes.

Finally, Ece popped out and waved at them. "Baths and food are ready. We can figure out the rest later." She had acquired normal clothes, but her hair was still disheveled.

They stepped up to the gatestone.

"Ready?" Ece asked. John tensed up and Cecil nodded. And then they were in House Husniye.

# 21

On seeing Ece, al-Haytham clapped with glee. She gave him a tired bow. "I'm back," she said, and he rushed forward to take her into a hug. Behind them, Ahu smiled at the exhausted group.

Then a voice called, "Ece?" and a throng of people burst into the gatestone room, all talking at once.

"Ece is back!"

"Cecil rescued her!"

John backed away from the cacophony. In the middle of the crowd, Ece, did her best to answer questions without crying. She must have mentioned him because John was suddenly surrounded.

"You rescued Ece?"

"When did you learn to move people through the gate network?"

"What happened?"

John gave Cecil a look of growing panic, and Cecil came to his rescue, helmet in the crook of his arm. "Hey, hey, ease up. He's been through a lot."

A woman near Ece cried, "Trey is dead?" and another uproar began.

"You killed Trey?" a petite woman yelped at Cecil's side. He nodded toward John. "He did, actually."

John held up his hands to fend off the eager crowd, but before he could speak, Ahmet's voice echoed through the gatestone room. "What is going on?"

The crowd parted as he stepped through the doorway, revealing Ece, who waved. Ahmet halted, eyes widening, he gasped. "Ece?"

Al-Haytham grinned slyly. "Yes, the operation to rescue Ece from Trey's grasp was successful. And the gatestone in Wetstone has been repaired."

Ahmet looked about, taking them in. "This is ... momentous. Cecil, congratulations! Wow. And Ece! You have Olumtahss around your neck! This is truly marvelous!"

Cecil saluted. "The operation was a success. We were both injured but walked away alive. Trey wasn't so lucky."

"Trey is dead?"

"Yessir."

Ahmet's smile slipped. "And you were brandishing Husniye's colors when you killed him? That will certainly ... send a message. Cecil, do you want to come to my office for a quick debrief?"

Al-Haytham spoke up. "They need to get their wounds looked at first. And Ece needs a bath." He waved his hand in front of his nose. Ece released an indignant cry. Laughter filled the room as they were whisked away, while others helped Cecil out of his armor. Reluctantly, John allowed himself to be pulled along.

Verifying that no one's wounds were serious, the crowd deposited them in a large, ornate room with a beautiful fountain in the center. John took in the lush benches and black-robed servants who were already placing snacks and drinks on tables. "This is the lounge for the bathhouse, right?"

"The hammam, yes." Cecil motioned for him to follow into a side room, already pulling his own clothes off. "Strip down, grab a towel, and meet us on the other side. Latrines are there if you need to use them."

Clad only in a towel, John opened the door to a hallway, lined with stone benches. Warmth from the next room enveloped him. Cecil waved him forward, and he stepped into the steam. Beside him, Cecil dropped his towel and sprawled nude atop a large stone in the center of the room. John sat gingerly, shuddering as he lowered himself onto the heated stone. Cecil pointed to the opposite end of the room, where a few muscular men waited next to a group of troughs. "Get cleaned up."

John nodded. Embarrassed and overwhelmed, but too tired to resist, John obeyed. He stepped into the trough, and the men sluiced him with warm water, then rubbed him down with cloths until his skin turned red. They cleaned and bandaged his wound. Just as John relaxed, Cecil tapped him on the shoulder.

"Let's go get some food."

John was suddenly aware of how hungry he was.

Now dressed in white robes, skin red from the heat, Cecil and John re-entered the lounge. Cool air feathered their faces as they sat on one of the luxuriously soft benches. The room had filled up with members of House Husniye, chattering among themselves.

Ece, lounging on another bench, called, "There's the man of the hour!" Bathed and shampooed, Ece's appearance and aroma had improved and the color returned to her skin. A heaping pile of food appeared before her, and she had already stained her white robe.

Ahu bowed. "Ece was just telling us about your skills with the bow."

"Thanks," John said.

"How did you get so good?"

"Well, if I missed, I wouldn't eat. So I learned not to miss."

Cecil raised a cup and called out, "We saved Ece, Trey is dead, and Olumtahss is ours again!" Ece held up the gatestone, and the crowd cheered.

Ahmet and al-Haytham interrupted their celebration. The bags under Ahmet's eyes looked like melting candles.

"Ece, I am glad you are back, but we need to do some damage control."

Ece sighed. "Ahmet, this can wait."

"No, it can't. We just killed the head of a house, and the Spire is upset about Olumtahss being back in our control."

Ece scowled at him. "The Spire is upset about ... Well, the Spire can suck a Twisted."

Ahmet winced. "Ece, this is serious."

"And it can wait until tomorrow."

"What should our public statement be, then? How in the world should we spin this?"

"Ahmet, I was kidnapped, and I haven't had a chance to properly rest or eat for quite some time, so I would really appreciate it if we handled this in the morning."

"Right, right, of course. I'll ... talk tomorrow."

Ece suddenly bolted upright, looking past Ahmet. "Yeela?"

Yeela had quietly crept into the room. She waved. "Hey, honey."

Ece panicked for a moment, mouth working, then regained her composure. Addressing the group, she said, "This is Yeela, a good friend of mine." To Yeela, "What are you doing here?"

"Actually, that's my doing," Cecil replied. "Someone kidnapped her to get at you, and I ended up rescuing her."

Ece was horrified. "They kidnapped you?"

"They did more than just that," Yeela said. She looked around before continuing. "White Masks." There was a collective gasp.

Yeela gave a dismissive wave. "Ece taught me a few tricks to keep my mind intact in case someone came knocking. It wasn't fun though." Her expression was something between a grin and a grimace.

Ahmet broke in. "Are you a mage?"

"In training," Yeela said, and when Ahmet turned to give Ece a dark look, she continued. "Perhaps she forgot to register me."

"I'll see what I can do," Ece said, noncommittal.

Yeela glared before breaking out into a mischievous grin. "It's a pretty funny story about how we met." John watched Ece's eyes go wide and her head shake as Yeela plowed ahead. "We met on Hydra Island."

Someone sniggered and was silenced with a shhh!

"She had hired me for a ... service but forgot to pay me. She bought me dinner later to make up for it, and we had a very pleasant time. Talked all night. Then, can you believe it, she hurried away to a meeting that morning and forgot to pay me again."

Ece's face had no expression, but she went red. The initial snicker escalated into full-blown laughter. Once the laughter died down, Yeela continued. "Eventually we made these dinners a regular occurrence, and she started teaching me magic."

Ahmet pounded the table with a fist. Those nearby jumped. "One more mess we'll have to deal with. Great."

Looking at Ece, Yeela snapped, "There is an easy way to fix that."

Ece averted her gaze and clenched her jaw.

"So after being kidnapped and tortured, I'm still not part of your life?"

Ece deflated, sinking into her chair. "Yeela …"

"Fuck you." Yeela turned to leave, then hesitated at the door. "I guess we can talk in the morning."

Cecil stood. "Well, it's been fantastic, but we are all exhausted. Let Ece get some sleep." He gave John a nod, and John rose to follow him. Ahu stepped forward to guide him to his room, where he collapsed onto the bed.

The next morning, John sat in his room, staring at the wall. He felt awkward wandering the halls alone, and al-Haytham was busy, or else John would have tried to grab a book. He answered a knock at the door. A serving woman directed, "Sir, if you could follow me?"

Grateful for something to do, he followed her. Eventually, they entered a large room, and John stopped cold.

Two men stood up, staring at him. They wore black tunics, black pants, and shiny shoes, all with purple trim.

Spire colors. One was dark-skinned with purple eyes and a shaved head, and the other painfully white skinned with black hair and brown eyes.

Behind the desk, Ahmet gestured, "Gentlemen, this is John. John, these are some representatives of the Spire."

John only had time to register Cecil slipping out the door before the pale one spoke. "A pleasure to meet you."

John said nothing.

The purple-eyed man leveled a gaze at him. "I believe we have some things to discuss about an incident in Wetstone."

"And what should I call you?" John asked.

The man smiled faintly, "You may call me sir, I suppose."

"How about Dave?" John said brightly. "May I call you Dave?" A look of annoyance crossed the man's face.

"One of Zen's little projects I see. You take after her," Purple Eyes said.

Ahmet cleared his throat. "John, why don't you have a seat and ..."

"Don't you dare hurt Zen," John blurted.

"That depends on how much you cooperate." Purple Eyes smiled.

"Oh, you want to make threats? Let's do threats. Let's talk about how you Spire assholes assassinated a head of a house and assisted another house in attempting a hostile takeover. I am sure if that got out things would get a little ... frosty around here."

"I don't know where you heard that."

Ahmet held up his hand. "Why don't we ..."

John barked, "She recorded it in Olumtahss before she died."

The Spire representatives stared. Ahmet's eyes bulged. He looked at the two men and stammered, "He … never mentioned that."

"I wonder what would happen if that became public knowledge," John said.

From the doorway, Ece spoke. "Yes, I wonder."

They all looked in her direction, and John saw Cecil give him a wave over her shoulder. He turned back to Ahmet, whose face was twitching.

"Hello, gentlemen. What are you doing here?" Ece asked.

Ahmet stood quickly and moved toward her. "We were just having a quick business meeting." He took her arm and tried to steer her back through the door.

She shook off his hand. "So you invited two official representatives of the Spire to a business meeting without informing the head of the house?"

"I was just … wrapping up some things really fast," Ahmet said.

"Wrapping up what, exactly?" Ece stepped around Ahmet. Both Cecil and Yeela followed her into the room.

"We were just discussing the incident in Wetstone," the pale one said. "Damaging a gatestone is a major crime."

"So is assassinating the head of a house," Ece replied.

John looked at Ahmet, whose face was a mask of pure horror. He took her arm again, saying, "Excuse us for a moment," as he tried to pull her off to one side. John saw Cecil's hand go to his sword.

Ahmet must have seen it too, because he looked at Cecil's expression, let go of Ece and leaned in to murmur,

"Listen, we all have personal feelings about this, but you need to keep a cool head."

"My head is very cool."

"We cannot afford to piss off the Spire."

Loud enough for the entire room to hear, Ece stated, "Husniye spent her whole life trying to appease the Spire and look where it got her."

Ahmet sighed. "You need to follow my lead on this. I hate to say it, but you were not Husniye's first choice for an heir. You don't have the experience to lead yet, as much as you want to. This is a very delicate situation, and we must tread softly." He emphasized the last three words.

"There is a reason Husniye didn't choose you to be the heir either, Ahmet." Ece whispered back, glaring at him. "Now sit down."

"Our house's lifeblood is the ink from merchant contracts. Please, Ece, do you want them to starve us out?"

"You would sell the heart of this house for a bit of coin."

"Having a heart doesn't feed people."

"Is money all you care about?"

"Oh, because you are famously good with money. You'll drive the house into bankruptcy within a week."

"I'm better with numbers than you are, and I don't make promises I can't keep," Ece retorted.

Ahmet glanced at Yeela, who had sidled next to John and was watching the whispered argument with interest. "What are you doing here?"

Yeela gave him a cheeky grin. "What do you mean? I am Ece's favorite consort, she pays me to follow her around."

It was Ece's turn to look horrified and glance at the Spire representatives. Neither reacted. Finally, she sputtered, "Yeela, now is not the best time for this."

"Oh, so when is?"

She took a breath, speaking quietly but quickly. "I didn't want you to be drawn into this. I didn't want you to be hurt, but I guess it happened anyway. I'm sorry I couldn't protect you. I'm sorry I abandoned you. I … I had plans to take you to Husniye, but I wanted to … get some things together first. I'm sorry."

Yeela wiped her eyes. Ahmet seemed frozen. John was doing his best to pretend he wasn't there, and it seemed Cecil was doing the same.

The pale representative coughed. "We can come back later, if that would be more convenient."

Ece turned to Ahmet. "What are they doing here?"

Ahmet regained his poker face. "To discuss loosening the restrictions the Spire has placed on the house."

"The Wetstone Consortium agreement," Ece stated.

"Yes, among others."

"And we just let them get away with this?"

Ahmet squirmed. "Officially, Trey did that," Ahmet whispered.

Ece squinted at him. "Were you the one who told them about John?"

"They figured it out. I don't know how. We just need to do damage control."

Ece turned her back on Ahmet and stepped forward. She took Ahmet's seat behind the desk and regarded the Spire representatives. "Well, gentlemen, it's nice to meet you. I have been informed that you have some paperwork we have been waiting on."

"I'm sorry?" Purple Eyes frowned

"The Wetstone Consortium contract, for one," Ece said.

"Ah, I assure you we will have it for you at the earliest convenience," he stated.

"It's convenient now. Do you need a pen?" Ece snatched one from the desk and held it toward the frowning men.

"You have the authority to sign it, right?"

"We need to discuss this with our peers," the man said.

"If you need a communication stone, you may use Olumtahss. Free of charge." Ece held out the red gem around her neck.

Purple Eyes stood abruptly, followed by Pale Guy. "We really can come back at a later time, if that's more convenient."

"There are two ways this can go," Ece said. "One involves you signing a contract."

John tried to blend into the wall as a dangerous silence permeated the room. Next to him, Cecil put on his best shit-eating grin.

Purple Eyes broke first. "Very well." He settled back into the chair, taking the pen. With trembling hands, Ahmet slapped a stack of papers in front of him.

He whipped through them, leaving behind a trail of glowing ink. The room was silent except for the rustling of paper and the scratch of the pen. Once he was done, he slapped the table and stood up. "We will be taking our leave now. John will be coming with us."

"Why does he need to go with you?" Ece asked.

Ahmet hissed, "Ece ..."

Purple Eyes leaned forward. "We have evidence that this man badly damaged a gatestone and murdered the head of a house."

Ece clicked her tongue. "Murdering the head of a house? That was self-defense! And what about the part where Trey kidnapped me and kept me in a cell?"

"Regardless, it's not your call. He broke the law and has to face consequences for it."

Ece put on a neutral face. "Do you have the paperwork?"

"Paperwork?"

"To arrest a member of a house. You need a written statement of the charges and where they will be held."

"He's a member of House Husniye?" Pale Guy pointed at John.

"Yes," Ece stated.

John saw Ahmet wince and Cecil grin.

"A gatestone was badly damaged," Purple Eyes insisted.

"An unfortunate accident." Ece shrugged.

Pale Guy raised an eyebrow. "The head of House DuFort is dead."

"A regrettable occurrence," Ece retorted.

"Is that so?"

"There have been many dreadful mishaps recently," Ece went on. "I think it's best just to move on, wouldn't you say?"

A long silence hung between Ece, John, and the men. Finally, Purple Eyes grunted, "Very well. I will speak with you later." They walked past John with barely a glance.

Once the door closed, Cecil gave John a slap on the back. "Welcome to House Husniye!" John let out the breath he was holding. Cecil put an arm around his shoulders and led him out of the room. "Let's get some paperwork filled out."

As they left, John heard Ahmet protesting. "You just had a lovers' spat in front of them, then burned every bit of goodwill we had left!"

Yeela snorted. "So I'm your lover now?"

"You are not part of this conversation." Ahmet pointed at her.

Ece lowered his hand. "Don't talk to her like that."

The door closed, but the muffled sounds of their argument followed John and Cecil down the hallway.

"That was fun. I am glad I fetched Ece."

"Thanks," John said.

"No problem. Did Husniye really leave some sort of record?"

"Maybe not exactly...." John said slyly.

Cecil laughed. "Let's make things official. Set you up with a bed and some duties. Does that sound good?"

John glanced at him. "I don't have a choice, do I?"

"Not really. I could try smuggling you to the church."

"Would Zen be in danger?"

Cecil nodded. "Probably. After Ece's stunt back there I am not sure how well that would go."

John stared at the ground, then nodded. "Yeah, I'll stay." He grinned at Cecil. "Not the worst fate."

Cecil roared with laughter. "Welcome to House Husniye."

# About the Author

I have always been a voracious reader. My childhood treat was going to a used bookstore to get a massive stack of used books to read. I always wanted to write my own story, and I wore a path in the bedroom carpet coming up with stories—really! I have continually had plots and ideas bouncing around in my head, with several faltering attempts to write them over the years. Eventually, I decided to "focus and finish," as my mom would say. This book is the result of a multi-year journey, one that started before AI was in the headlines, and one that was far harder than I thought it would be. Enjoy!

**Email:** bradford.renwick.kuhn@gmail.com